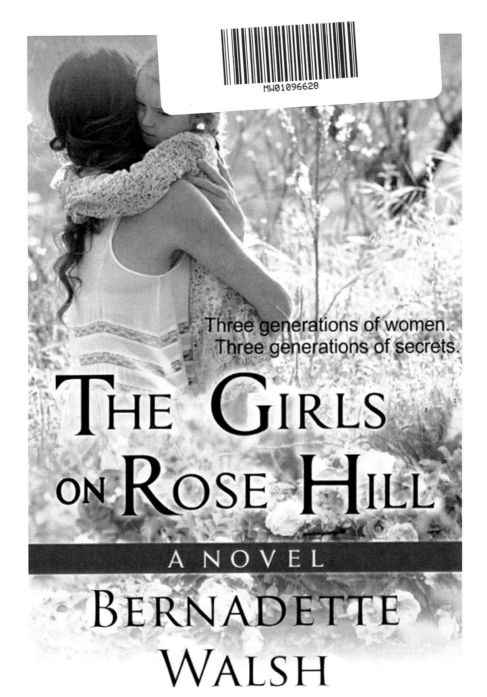

Three generations of women.
Three generations of secrets.

THE GIRLS
ON ROSE HILL

A NOVEL

BERNADETTE
WALSH

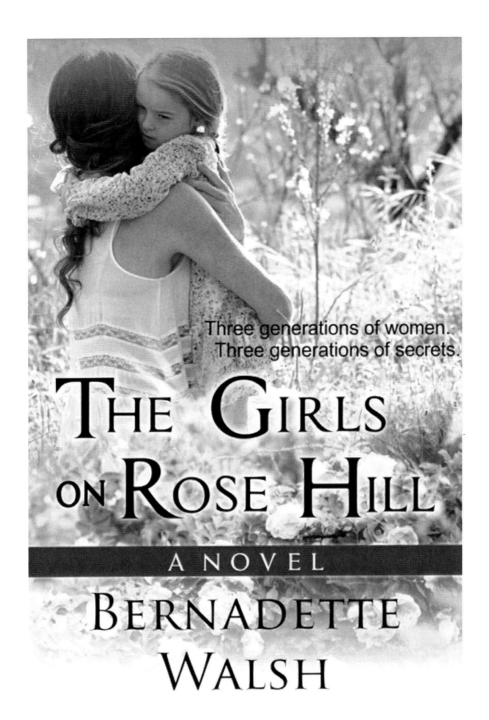

Three generations of women.
Three generations of secrets.

THE GIRLS
ON ROSE HILL

A NOVEL

BERNADETTE
WALSH

The Girls on Rose Hill
A Novel

by

Bernadette Walsh

By payment of required fees, you have been granted the *non*-exclusive, *non*-transferable right to access and read the text of this eBook. No part of this text may be reproduced, transmitted, downloaded, decompiled, reverse engineered, or stored in or introduced into any information storage and retrieval system, in any form or by any means, whether electronic or mechanical, now known or hereinafter invented without the express written permission of copyright owner.

Please Note

This is a work of fiction. Names, characters, places, and incidents either are the product of the author's imagination or are used fictitiously, and any resemblance to actual persons, living or dead, business establishments, events or locales is entirely coincidental.

The reverse engineering, uploading, and/or distributing of this eBook via the internet or via any other means without the permission of the copyright owner is illegal and punishable by law. Please purchase only authorized electronic editions, and do not participate in or encourage electronic piracy of copyrighted materials. Your support of the author's rights is appreciated.

eBook design by eBook Prep www.ebookprep.com

Chapter 1

Rose

The noon sun blinded me and it was all I could do not to turn around and crawl back into bed. I was tired. Bone tired as my mother used to say. I rummaged through the straw basket and found a scratched pair of plastic sunglasses my granddaughter left behind last summer. I grabbed the thin iron railing and made my way down the porch's steep steps one step at a time, the way my mother had in her last few years. Old. I was getting old. I'd flown up and down these stairs since I was a child but last month I missed the third step and twisted my ankle. Now, like my mother before me, I had to be careful.

I peered through the damaged glasses. My brother's anchored sailboat bobbed merrily in the high tide. In the distance, several men fished off of the Centershore bridge, their low murmurs carried by a light breeze. One of the men wiped his bald head with a rag. A small bead of sweat trickled down my own brow. Summer used to be my favorite season but this month's string of ninety degree days had sapped my energy.

I walked over to the shed, painted the same robin's egg blue as the house, and hesitated, almost involuntarily, before I stepped inside the dank, termite ridden structure. The sharp tang of fertilizer mixed with kerosene still reminded me of my stepfather. Sixty years on, I could almost see his broad shoulders block the narrow doorway, his thin lips a hard line. I shook my head and forced the image out of my mind. A stepladder lay just inside the shed's door. I dragged it out into the sun and over to a large lilac bush. Although it was June, a few flowering branches remained. They would make a nice addition to St. Ann's mid-week altar arrangement.

"Hello, Rose," Barbara Conroy said. Barbara and her late husband had lived next door for close to forty years. I couldn't remember the last time our greetings had extended beyond a hello and a weather observation. Yet as a long time neighbor, Barbara's habits and schedule were as familiar as my own. Barbara carried a tray of sandwiches for her weekly historical society meeting.

I forced a smile. "Hi, Barbara. Hot enough for you?"

"It's brutal." She placed the tray in the back seat of her new silver Mercedes. Since her husband died last spring, Barbara had enjoyed spending all the pennies he'd pinched over their long marriage.

I waved one last time to Barbara and turned my attention to the lilacs. Every Wednesday I freshened the altar's flower arrangements, although attendance at the daily masses was sparse. Still, Monsignor Ryan appreciated my efforts.

I wiped my sweaty palms on the faded housedress my daughter tried to throw out last summer and then grabbed the heavy gardening shears out of the straw basket. I climbed to the top of the stepladder and reached for a large unwilted blossom. As I lifted the shears over my head, a sharp pain pierced my skull. The gardening shears fell to the ground. I shouldn't have gone out in this heat, I thought as I climbed down the ladder. I reached the last step when another flash of pain, stronger than the last, ripped through my head. Then darkness.

* * *

Two weeks later I found myself installed in a small single room at St. Francis Hospice. Invasive brain cancer. No treatment options. No hope. Three months at most. It seemed I'd meet the Lord a little sooner than I'd expected.

"I said, do you want me to put more water in this vase?" my sister-in-law Lisa shouted in my left ear.

"Sorry, yes. That's fine," I said, my voice, despite my effort, no louder than a whisper.

"These are pretty. Are they from your garden?" Lisa asked loudly as she walked to the small adjoining bathroom.

I wanted to tell her I had cancer, I wasn't deaf. Instead I replied, "Yes. Ellen brought them yesterday." My daughter, Ellen, had brought offerings from my garden every day since she'd arrived from Washington. If I live much longer, there won't be a blade of grass left.

"Well, she certainly didn't cut them very well, but then Ellen was never one for flowers, was she?" Lisa bustled back into the room and a small stream of water dripped from an overfilled vase. "I

5

can't believe she's staying all alone at your place. Paul and I told her she was more than welcome to stay with us. The kids are away at camp this month so there's plenty of room. But no, she said she wanted to spend time at home. I was surprised to hear her call it that. Home. When was the last time she was back anyway?"

"I don't remember," I lied as I looked out the small window next to my bed. The window faced a small courtyard with a statue of Our Lady in the center, surrounded by a bed of day lilies. A young woman placed a small bouquet of flowers at Our Lady's feet.

"I don't think she's been back twice since Kitty died. I would've thought that she considered D.C. her home now. Not like Paul. He's always loved that old house. He was born there after all," Lisa added as if I didn't know.

"So was Ellen." I looked at the young woman praying in the courtyard, her dark hair a curtain across her face. The bright orange of the day lilies was like fire against her black hair as the blossoms danced in the breeze. I stared at the flowers and an image of my Auntie Margaret's back yard in Bay Ridge flashed across my damaged brain.

Margaret's front yard, like that of her Brooklyn neighbors, consisted of a small postage stamp lawn. All proper and controlled. In the back she'd created a magic garden for me and my cousin Molly. Paths lined with rows of beautiful wildflowers criss-crossed the small yard and bright orange day lilies softened the back fence. We would hide for hours among the flowers. Molly and I crept along the rough wooden fence, orange blossoms caught in our hair, the day my mother and Peter came to take me to the house on Rose Hill.

My hands were covered in dirt and Auntie Margaret tried to rub them clean with a soft handkerchief, her eyes red with tears. My mother stood next to a strange man. He was tall with a large nose and enormous hands. My mother handed him a small suitcase and then hugged me. My grubby fingers stained her pale green dress. "Rosie, I have the best news. You have a new daddy, and we're going to take you with us to live in a beautiful house by the sea. Isn't that marvelous? Aren't you the luckiest girl in the world?"

"Are we going on vacation? Can Molly come too?"

"Of course Molly will visit us. But no, this isn't a vacation. You're coming to live with me. With us," Kitty said, in a bright, chirpy voice.

6

"But I live here," I said, bewildered. "I live with Auntie Margaret and Uncle John and Molly and baby Jack."

"Yes, you did live here. Now you're going to live with your own mommy and daddy," Kitty said, her voice hardened as she glared at Auntie Margaret.

I looked at the sour-faced man. "But I don't know him. I don't like him!"

The man glanced at his watch as if he hadn't heard a word I'd said. Tears slid down my cheeks.

Auntie Margaret took me in her arms. "Hush now, child," she said in her soft brogue. "There's no reason to cry. You'll love your new home with your mammy. And we'll all come out to visit you soon."

"Kitty, we need to go," the man said.

Without another word, my mother lifted me up in her arms and carried me out of the yard. I looked back through my tears. Auntie Margaret crouched down beside my cousin Molly, Margaret's black hair framed against the fire of the day lilies.

Lisa's grating voice brought me back to the hospice room. "...and so I offered to send my gardener over to your place, but Ellen wouldn't hear of it. Really, it's no problem. After all, she'll need to get back to Washington, to her job and her family soon I would think, and someone will need to take care of the house. Paul and I would be happy to do it." Lisa squeezed my thin hand in her plump one.

"Happy to do what?" Ellen asked from the doorway.

"Ellen, I didn't see you there. I was just telling Rose that our gardener would be happy to take care of Rose's garden. It's no problem."

"This is neither the time nor the place to discuss the garden, Lisa. My mother shouldn't be bothered with such details," Ellen said in what I always thought of as her lawyer voice.

"I was only trying to help." Lisa then turned to me and said in a louder voice, "Rose, you must be tired. I'll see you tomorrow."

"Good bye, Lisa," I said. "God bless."

Lisa was barely out the door when Ellen sat on my bed and said, "God, what a vulture. Could she be more obvious? She and Paul practically live in a mansion and she can't wait to get her fat mitts on your place. Honestly, I don't know how Paul can stand her."

7

"She means well."

"You always say that," Ellen said, irritation lacing her words. "For years you've said she means well. What does that even mean? And why does she shout at you?"

"I don't know."

"Because she's an idiot, that's why. God, let's stop talking about her. I didn't come here to bitch about Lisa again." Ellen walked over to the window. "It's a nice, bright room anyway."

"Yes. It's got a lovely garden."

"Maybe if you're up for it we can go there tomorrow. Oh, and your friend is down there." Ellen gestured toward the statue of Our Lady.

"I know, it's a comfort." I paused and then against my better judgment added, "She could be your friend too, Ellen."

"It's a little late for me." Ellen took in a deep breath, like she always did when she wanted to control her temper. I'd say what I thought was something innocuous and not likely to set her off, Ellen would snap at me, I'd backtrack and take back whatever offensive word escaped my mouth, she'd get more annoyed. We'd danced this dance for years now. Ever since Ellen hit school and realized that it wasn't normal to live with your grandmother, your uncles and your awkward, ex-nun mother. The house on Rose Hill may have had a white picket fence, but that was about the only thing about it that was normal. My Ellen spent her childhood keeping up with Joneses in our affluent town, and the Joneses didn't have mothers like me. Mothers who didn't come paired with fathers. Mothers who kept secrets from their daughters.

But now that her pathetic excuse for a mother had come down with cancer, the "bad kind" as my mother would say, Ellen had managed to control her temper. For the most part anyway, although her constant tongue-biting was unnerving.

Ellen sat on the chair beside my bed. Her normally glossy blonde hair showed an inch of gray roots and her high cheekbones were sharper than usual, as if she'd lost weight too quickly. It was strange to see my elegant daughter look anything but perfect. To distract her I asked, "When is Veronica due in?"

Ellen smiled for the first time all day. "Tomorrow morning. Her train should be in around eleven. We'll stop by here in the afternoon."

8

"Good." My eyelids felt like lead. "Good."

Chapter 2

Ellen

The morning breeze was cool. Thank God the heat wave finally broke. One more night in my mother's sweat box of a house and I swear I'd drown myself in the Long Island Sound.

The salt-tinged breeze washed over me as I sat on the front porch and drank coffee out of Granny's favorite red mug. What would Granny Kitty say if she could see me sprawled on her front steps in my wrinkled shorts? She'd probably drag me inside the kitchen, the proper place for drinking coffee, and harass me until I put on something decent.

But Kitty wasn't here, nor was Rose, and with only my daughter Veronica with me, I was now the matriarch of the house. Oddly giddy at the thought, I wondered if there were any other house rules I could break, as though I was thirteen and not forty-three. I savored my strong coffee, so unlike the hospital's watery concoctions, and watched two young boys from the local yachting club maneuver their sailboat under the Centershore bridge. The briny wind carried he taller one's little boy curses.

I looked at the diamond watch my husband bought me last year. Only an hour until I was due back at the hospice center and the weeds and flowers weren't about to pick themselves. I looked at the little boys again. How I wished I could climb into the boat with them and sail away from mother and this old house and the hospital stench that seemed to have become permanently lodged in my nostrils. Unfortunately an escape from this particular unpleasant chapter of my life would not be so easy.

I picked up the battered gardening basket I'd bought my mother many birthdays ago, walked to the rose bushes that lined the walkway and cut the few remaining intact flowers. My grandmother had told my mother when they had first moved to Centerport that she'd planted the rose bushes in honor of the five-year-old Rose, and that the winding lane, Rose Hill, was named in Rose's honor. For years my mother believed my grandmother until a neighbor told her old Mrs. Frohller, Kitty's mother-in-law, had planted the roses long before Rose was born and long before Mrs. Frohller's son Peter ever met the pretty Irish widow. Still, as Mrs. Frohller's rose bushes eventually withered and died, Kitty, and then Rose, replaced them and tended the rose bushes with care.

If my mother and grandmother had each been blessed with a green thumb then I'd been cursed with a black one. In the two weeks my mother'd been at St. Francis, I'd managed to kill three spider plants and the ficus in the hallway didn't look too healthy. If my mother could see me awkwardly hack at the roses, she'd gently admonish me in that pained way she had whenever someone other than herself handled her treasured flowers. Well, she's not here to see, I thought grimly. I reached for a large yellow blossom and impaled my thumb on a thorn.

"Shit." I brought my bleeding thumb to my mouth.

"Are you okay?" My daughter asked in a sleepy voice behind me.

I laughed and turned to face her. "Yeah. I was attacked by a flower." I arranged my features into the face I usually presented to my children—that of a cheerful, competent, loving mother—and smiled. "Are you hungry? I have fruit and yogurt in the kitchen."

Veronica ran her fingers through her unruly auburn curls. "Oh, Mom, I could really use a bagel."

I handed her the straw basket. "Okay, you take this inside and I'll make a bagel run."

I shook the dirt from my hands before I opened the door of my new silver German sedan. After years of driving squat sexless mini-vans with their three row seats and sensible beverage holders, I'd finally treated myself to one of the sleek expensive cars my husband Brendan favored. With Veronica soon off to NYU and the twins safely tucked away in their top-tier colleges, I no longer needed to cart around hockey skates, lacrosse sticks or gaggles of giggling cheerleaders. When Brendan complained about the price, I told him I'd served my time and deserved some comfort and style. Guilt always opened his wallet.

A half hour later, after she'd convinced me to cook her a full breakfast, Veronica dug into a plate of scrambled eggs and bacon. My twenty-year old twin boys, Michael and Timothy, older than

Veronica by eighteen months, had inherited my heavy blonde locks but there was no doubt that this red-haired sprite was my daughter. We both shared my grandmother Kitty's cornflower blue eyes and curvy figure and we both had the wide set eyes and high cheekbones donated by Mr. Mystery, which was how Kitty had always referred to my unknown father.

"More tea?" I asked.

"Please." Like the Queen of England, Veronica held out her mug while I poured. My Granny always called Veronica a "right little madam" and I supposed she was. My fault, of course. I'd indulged Veronica and used the excuse of our "girl time" to escape my rowdy sons and inattentive husband—weekend trips to dance competitions, shopping at Georgetown's nearby high end boutiques and, of course, our weekly mani-pedi sessions. The housekeeper still made her bed and I wasn't sure Veronica even knew where the washing machine was. My pampered daughter was in for a rude awakening next year at college.

Ah, who was I kidding? I was the one who'd be in for a rude awakening. After twenty years of the welcome distractions provided by three children, I'd be left alone with an enormous house and an even more enormous emotional gulf between myself and Brendan, who, to be honest, felt more like a slightly annoying roommate than a husband.

Unaware of my traitorous thoughts about her father, Veronica sipped her tea and stared out the small kitchen window. "Mom, what's going on back there?"

I'd managed to keep the front garden somewhat in check, but hadn't touched the backyard which, in this heat, was overrun with weeds. Lisa was right, I did need the help of the gardener to maintain my mother's horticultural paradise. I could probably use one in the house too since the ficus was clearly on its last leg. However, I'd kill every plant in Centerport rather than admit Lisa was right. Stubborn. I'd always been stubborn, a trait my Granny always said I must've inherited from Mr. Mystery rather than my meek mother.

"I know, it's a mess. Maybe you can help me weed later."

Veronica made a face. "I thought we were clearing out the master bedroom today."

I patted her crimson curls. "That too. Put the dishes in the sink when you're done and meet me upstairs."

"Mom," she whined, "I need a shower."

I stifled the urge to pinch Veronica on the inside of her arm the way my Granny had always done whenever I was sulky and fresh. I said with more good humor than I felt, "After your shower then," and then walked out of the kitchen, past the remnants of the ficus in the hallway and up the stairs.

I looked at my watch again. Eleven o'clock. My mother should've finished her final dose of chemo by now. Although I'd offered to accompany her, my mother insisted she only wanted her cousin Molly with her. She used Veronica being here as an excuse, and I didn't push. I was relieved, to tell the truth. To assuage my guilt, I decided to search through my mother's belongings and find some photos to hang in her hospice room.

Even after my grandmother died five years ago, my mother continued to sleep in the same narrow bedroom facing the back garden she'd occupied for most of her sixty-five years. Her bedroom was as neat and spare as I imagine her postulant's room at Our Lady of Angels convent was so many years earlier. It's only adornment was a crucifix and a small copy of my wedding portrait.

Across the hall, the master bedroom was the house's largest and brightest bedroom, and the only one with a view of Centerport harbor. About a year after my grandmother died, I made one of my rare trips home and forced my mother to organize Kitty's clothes and donate what was salvageable to St. Ann's. I urged my mother to get rid of the rest of Kitty's things and move into the larger and more comfortable bedroom. My mother nodded and agreed with me while I was here, but clearly hadn't been in the room since, except to store a few boxes. Kitty's ring, watch and hairbrush sat on the nightstand next to the bed and the room still had a slight scent of Kitty's musky perfume.

I opened the bottom drawer of a large cherry armoire stuffed with envelopes. My nose twitched from the musty smell. I opened the first envelope and found a letter from my great grandmother Eileen, my namesake. The rest of the letters were from various members of Granny Kitty's family back in Ireland, although most were from her mother Eileen. I tried the next drawer and came up with a large package. Inside was a letter from my grandmother's brother, Danny, who had inherited Templeglantin, the family farm in

County Kerry. After Eileen's death Danny returned to Kitty the letters she had written to her mother over the years.

All of this was interesting, but I didn't think my mother would find these musty old letters particularly uplifting. My mother wasn't one to linger on the past. I was the one who loved to hear my grandmother's stories about Ireland. Behind Granny's back, Mom would roll her eyes. Never to Granny's face, though. My meek mother wasn't that brave. Honestly, I wasn't sure what would cheer my mother up. Her friends from the Rosary Society had plastered her room with enough prayer cards and bloody pictures of the Sacred Heart to cause even the Pope lose his lunch. Her room was already full of flowers. Other than flowers and Jesus, my mother didn't have too many other interests. At least none that I knew of. Still, I had to try and do something to lift her spirits. God knows our stilted conversations hadn't cheered her up. After a half hour in each other's company, she'd stare out the window biting her lip and I'd have a migraine.

I hit pay dirt when I found an old photo album with Margaret O'Connor Sullivan written in faded ink on the inside cover. Margaret died when I was a baby, but I knew how close my mother was to her aunt.

"Find anything?" Veronica asked pleasantly, the shower having improved her mood.

"Mostly old letters. But I did find this album." I flipped through the pages. "Look, here's a picture of my grandfather."

"He was handsome."

"Kitty always said that Tim Murphy from Monaghan was the most beautiful man she ever saw."

Veronica pointed to a picture of Tim with his arms around a petite dark haired woman. "Hey, that's not Granny Kitty, is it?"

"No, that's Auntie Margaret." I turned another page to find Tim and Margaret holding hands at Coney Island.

Veronica idly twisted one of her damp curls around her finger as she lay sprawled across Kitty's bed. "She looks just like Nana. Those two look very chummy, don't they?"

"Oh, didn't I tell you? He used to be engaged to Auntie Margaret."

"Get out!" Veronica sat up. "You never told me that."

"I didn't? Well, that's probably because Kitty didn't like to talk about it, and neither did my mother. I only found out from one of my cousins at a family wedding a few years ago."

"So you've never seen these pictures?" Veronica asked.

"Nope, and I'm surprised Kitty didn't burn them. She never had anything good to say about Margaret. Here's a picture of Kitty and Margaret on Kitty's wedding day."

"Why is Margaret carrying a bouquet? Oh my God, she wasn't the bridesmaid, was she?"

"Apparently."

"This is better than a soap opera." Veronica jumped off the bed to get a better look. "How did Kitty wind up with Tim anyway?"

"That was a bit of a scandal. Kitty used to work in a bar."

"Granny Kitty worked in a bar? Miss 'tanks tops are not appropriate clothing for young ladies'? Miss 'red nail polish looks cheap'? I don't believe you."

Veronica had only known my grandmother when she was ancient; gnarled with arthritis and, near the end, crippled by dementia. The thought of Granny Kitty serving drinks and flirting with brawny Irishman was obviously a bit shocking to my daughter. I ruffled Veronica's hair. "Before she became a practical nurse, Kitty was a bar maid. I believe she was very popular."

"Well, look at her." Veronica pointed to the wedding picture. "Even in those awful clothes, she was pretty hot." The faded black and white photo couldn't hide Kitty's dazzling wide smile and luscious hour glass figure.

Veronica held up a picture of Tim and Kitty kissing next to a Christmas tree. "Can you believe that these two people produced Nana? I know that sounds mean, and you know how much I love Nana, but come on. These two are smoking and Nana, well, she's just not."

"Smoking or not, your grandmother's always been very good to you. And we're supposed to find some happy, uplifting pictures. Pictures of dead people, no matter how hot, are not what your grandmother needs right now. I can't believe you forgot to bring up my photo albums. I promised Molly we'd meet her at St. Francis by two, so let's just do the best we can. You go through those boxes by the window while I try another one of these drawers."

"Okay," Veronica said with a dramatic sigh. She clearly wanted to hear more about her great grandparents' racy love triangle rather than do any work. But, at heart Veronica was a good girl and despite her penchant for heavy sighs and eye rolls, was generally compliant.

I sifted through the old chest's drawers and found another of Margaret's photo albums. This one contained baby photos of her own three children and pictures of Rose from age eighteen months to age five. After my grandfather Tim Murphy was crushed by a collapsed brick wall at a building site, Kitty became a live-in practical nurse and worked for wealthy elderly matrons in Manhattan. Since Kitty couldn't take a baby with her to the sickrooms, she'd left Rose with her sister Margaret, who in the interim had married a widowed police sergeant and was pregnant herself. If Margaret resented being saddled with the child of her former fiancé and her flirty sister, it didn't show in these pictures. There were several faded photos of a very pregnant Margaret holding Rose quite tenderly. Rose shared Margaret's dark straight hair, small narrow face and pointed chin and looked more like Margaret's child than the chubby fair haired Molly who was born soon thereafter. I found a picture of Rose, age five, holding Molly's hand, surrounded by a sea of daffodils. I carefully removed the snapshot from Margaret's album.

"Any luck?" I asked Veronica.

"Here's a photo of Nana dressed up like a nun, but it's weird, it doesn't look like she's at a Halloween party."

"Let me see. I've never seen a picture of my mother in her veil."

"Her veil?"

"Your grandmother spent six months in a convent when she was seventeen." The photo of a young Rose smiling broadly in her short blue postulant's veil made me smile myself. My mother looked so happy, even joyful, that her normally pinched features were almost beautiful.

"What other family secrets haven't you told me?" Veronica scolded. "Am I adopted? Is Dad secretly an alien?"

I laughed and ruffled her hair again. "Your father is many things, but an alien he is not. Nana didn't really tell me too much about her convent days. Besides it was so long ago, I never thought

16

to tell you. This is such a great photo and I'm sure she hasn't seen it in a while. Let's add it to the pile. Did you find anything else?"

"I found her high school graduation picture, but she looks kind of nervous."

"No, I only want pictures where she's smiling, happy."

Veronica sifted through some more photos and then handed me a small, creased photo. "What about this one, Mom? Nana's smiling and it looks like she's at a party."

In the photo Molly and her husband Bobby, dressed in his police cadet's uniform, stood next to my mother and another young cadet. My mother's normally straight hair was ratted in a sixties bouffant and she had a full face of makeup. Both of the young men held beers. I flipped the picture over and read the faded scrawl: St. Paddy's Day, 1966. Me, Bobby, Rosie and Denis.

"St. Patrick's Day, 1966," I said. I stared at the picture of the young cadet named Denis. He was blond, with high cheek bones. Very wide set eyes.

"Mom, what is it?"

"Nothing, sweetie. Why don't you finish getting dressed and then we'll head over to St. Francis."

After Veronica left the room I sat on Kitty's high four-poster bed. I looked at the photo again, and focused only on the fair, handsome young man. I was born on December 20th, 1966. "Dear God," I said aloud, "I think this man is my father."

Chapter 3

Ellen

I'd placed the last of the newly framed photos on my mother's bedside tables when my mother's cousin, Molly, walked in. Her broad face was pale and her light blue eyes dull with fatigue, but she brightened when she noticed Veronica.

"This can't be Veronica." Molly's meaty arms engulfed my daughter in a bear hug. "Last time I saw you, you were playing with your dollies."

Veronica grinned. "I left them in the car."

"You look fantastic, Veronica. So grown up. Rose tells me you'll be at NYU this fall."

"That's right. I can't wait to get out of boring Washington. I love Manhattan, especially Greenwich Village."

"Now that you're local I expect to see a lot more of you, young lady," Molly mock scolded. "I know Sarah will be happy that you'll be close by." Sarah was Molly's change of life baby and only girl after four boys.

"She still has one more year at Queen of the Rosary Academy, right, Molly?" I asked.

"Yes, she'll be a senior."

"Has she decided on a college yet?" I asked.

"It changes daily." Molly barely glanced in my direction. She then turned back to Veronica and said, "Maybe you could give her some ideas."

"I'd love to, Aunt Molly."

"Those are beautiful roses, Veronica," Molly said. "They should cheer your grandmother right up."

"Thanks. Mom and I wanted to do something to brighten the room. We even brought some photos." Veronica pointed to the two side tables that flanked the high hospital bed.

Molly walked over and picked up a picture of Rose and my three kids taken in front of my house in Georgetown. She smiled and

18

then looked at a picture of Rose and my uncle Paul taken ten years ago on his first sailboat. "My God, I almost forgot that Paul used to have hair." Molly then picked up the photo of Rose in her postulant's habit. "What is this?"

"I found it in Kitty's room. Isn't it a great photo? Mom looks so happy in it."

"I don't think she'll want to see this." Molly snatched the photo off the table. She then looked at the photo of herself and Rose as children in her mother's back yard. "This will have to go as well. Ellen, why on earth did you drag these here? Why were you poking through your mother's things? Couldn't you have the decency to wait until she's dead?"

"Veronica," I said, "please go down to the cafeteria and get us some coffee." For once Veronica didn't object, and scooted out of the room.

I forced myself to remain calm. Molly had a trigger temper, and I'd learned from experience that Molly didn't respond well to confrontation. "What's wrong with these photos, Molly? I think they're nice. They'll cheer Mom up."

"Cheer her up? Good God, Ellen, do you not know your mother at all? Rose was devastated when Kitty dragged her home from the convent. And this picture of us as children? It was taken when Rosie used to live with us. You have to know Rose was traumatized when Kitty ripped her from our family."

"What are you talking about? This is the first I'm hearing this."

"Well, you always were Kitty's girl, weren't you? Never gave your poor mother the time of the day. We've hardly seen you these past five years. If you don't know the most basic facts of your mother's life, you've only yourself to blame." Molly grabbed my arm. "But listen to me, Ellen, and listen good. You can't upset her now. The doctors said this morning they'd be surprised if she makes it past this month. So stick a smile on your face and talk about the weather. But don't bring up the past and, for heaven's sake, leave these moldy old pictures at home."

Despite my good intentions, I opened my purse and pulled out the St. Paddy's Day picture. "You mean pictures like this? If I don't know the most basic facts of my mother's life as you say, it's because she refused to share them. I begged her to tell me who my father was. Of course she wouldn't tell me. Kitty, my uncles, the whole

19

family acted like I was the result of an immaculate conception. But look, here he is."

Molly's fair cheeks flamed. "Show some respect, Ellen. Now is neither the time nor the place."

"It is obvious that this is my father. You know who he is. Don't bother denying it."

"Ellen, I..."

The door swung open. "Now, here we are Miss Murphy." A tall, young male aide pushed a gurney into the room. My mother's eyes were half closed, her face drawn and gray.

Molly rushed to her side, "Rosie, sweetheart, we're here. Myself and Ellen."

The aide settled my frail mother in the bed. A few moments later Veronica entered the room with a tray of coffees. I didn't want to alarm either my mother or my daughter so I forced myself to calm down. I sat next to Veronica and sipped my coffee while Molly and the aide straightened the bedcovers. After the aide left, Molly sat closest to my mother. She gently stroked my mother's thin hair and murmured a string of words. Nothing important really, just something to let my mother know, in her drugged state, that she wasn't alone. That she was loved.

The lines around Molly's eyes seemed to have deepened during these past two weeks, and her normally full face was slack. Ever since I was a teenager, and hell maybe even before that, Molly had made it painfully clear she didn't think much of me. Unlike the rest of the family, she wasn't impressed by my straight As or homecoming queen good looks. But, then again, Molly didn't think much of my grandmother either.

At my grandmother's wake, unlike the rest of the extended O'Connor/Murphy/Frohller clan, Molly's eyes were dry. Near the end of the night, when I was in the ladies' room trying to repair my mascara, she stood behind me and said into the mirror, "Well, Rosie's free of her. Free of her at last."

"What in God's name are you talking about? My mother's destroyed. Absolutely destroyed by this."

"I'll admit she's been destroyed. Destroyed by that selfish woman."

"I don't know what you're talking about," I spat. "Everyone loved Kitty. Most of all my mother."

Molly stared at me in the mirror for a few moments. Her angry face softened and she said in a more conciliatory tone, "Ellen, I know that you're busy with the children." She placed her hand on my arm. "But, please come home more often. Your mother needs you."

"I just lost my grandmother," I said, my tears flowed again. "I can't talk about this."

The few times I'd seen Molly since, we were nominally polite and kept our distance. But I couldn't deny that Molly had been good to my mother over the years. She included her in family gatherings like Sunday dinners at Molly's large colonial in neighboring Huntington. In recent years, since Molly's husband Bobby died, they even vacationed together. They were closer than most sisters and these past three weeks had taken their toll on the usually unflappable Molly. Despite our differences over the years, even I had to feel sorry for her. Although I should be ashamed to admit it, I suspected she'd feel the loss of my mother more than I would.

"Molly," I said, "you must be exhausted. Why don't you go home and get some sleep? Veronica and I can stay with her until Paul comes in from work."

Molly nodded. She kissed Rose's forehead and left without looking at me. This morning's chemo session and our little altercation had clearly exhausted Molly. I was exhausted as well. I sat beside my mother and stroked her thin hand as she slept.

Chapter 4

Ellen

"Girls, come on," I shouted up the stairs. "You're going to miss your flight." The girls giggled in reply. After my semi-altercation with Molly, Veronica offered to cancel her graduation trip to Italy, but I wouldn't let her. Veronica and her friend Hailey were meeting up with their friend Alison Shanley and her parents. Alison's mother, Nancy, had been a Bunco friend of mine before I went back to work. And before my husband Brendan flirted with her in full view of all my friends. Allison and I still had a very cordial relationship. If I stopped talking to every woman in D.C. Brendan had either slept with or wanted to sleep with, I'd practically be a mute.

The girls were originally scheduled to fly out of Dulles with the Shanleys, but after my mother got sick we changed Veronica's ticket and Veronica convinced Hailey to do the same. I think she could convince Hailey to chug bleach if she wanted to. Well, there are leaders and there are followers in this world and my little red haired daughter was definitely a leader. She wasn't mean spirited about it and generally didn't abuse her power over her band of followers. Veronica was blessed with her father's natural charisma. Fortunately, in her case, that charisma was tempered by a tender heart.

Honestly, I was relieved to see Veronica go. Ever since I found that photo, all I wanted to do was tear the house apart and search for clues about Mr. Mystery's identity. Instead, I'd spent the last two days entertaining Veronica and her sidekick. Their happy teenaged chatter grated on my already frayed nerves but I smiled through it.

"Veronica, the car's here." I ordered a car to take the girls to JFK because my uncle Danny and I were on Rose duty this weekend. Molly was in Boston for her daughter-in-law's baby shower and Paul and Lisa had a wedding out on the East End of Long Island. Rose perked up a bit a day or so after her final chemo session, but it was clear the end was near. If I was a good daughter, I'd put this whole unknown father thing out of my mind and focus on the parent I did have. The parent who needed me. But, as Molly could attest, I'd never been a good daughter.

I wasn't sure why that was exactly. Before I started school, I'd adored my mother. She would spend hours plaiting my hair and playing dolls. Rose never yelled or nagged me to put my coat on. She was more like a big sister than a mother. It wasn't until first grade that I noticed Rose was unlike all the other mothers, with their perfectly coiffed hair and their heels and lipstick; mothers like Barbara Conroy. Rose wore her hair in a nun-like page boy, her jet black hair lank and stick-straight. Her clothes were anything but fashionable. As I looked back on it now, Rose had tried to fit in. She volunteered for every committee, and one year she was even a class mother, but she was ill at ease among the wealthy suburban matrons, most of whom were her senior by several years. By third grade, I'd managed to lose the notices asking for volunteers and whenever I needed to be dropped off at a birthday party or girl scout function, I'd ask Kitty to take me. Kitty was close enough in age to some of the older mothers, but more importantly, with her bright blond hair, stylish clothes and easy laugh, she fit right in. Kitty became quite popular with the other mothers, and was old enough that the other mothers viewed her flirty ways as endearing rather than threatening.

So little by little, Kitty took over more of the public parenting role while Rose slowly faded into the background. That's not to say that we didn't have a relationship of sorts. Rose always made sure that I ate healthy food since if it was up to Kitty I would've lived on tea and chocolate biscuits. Rose was also very attentive to my school work and would spend hours with me working on book reports and science projects. But when it came to the fun stuff, like discussing who to invite to my next birthday party or what to wear to a dance, I turned to Kitty.

Of course as I got older and figured out that, while I may have been a "little gift from heaven" as my mother liked to tell me, my origins were likely less celestial, my relationship with my mother became more rocky. Regardless of how many ways I posed the question, she never provided even a hint as to who my father was and the circumstances of my conception. Hell, my mother was so buttoned up about anything even remotely sexual that she could barely say the word "tampon." I would cry, whine, yell, but nothing I did could penetrate my mother's impassive silence. I was so angry with her after yet another one of her refusals to tell me about my father, I accepted a scholarship to Boston College despite her objections and forged her signature on the paperwork. At the end of that summer I left for Boston and then four years later for Georgetown Law School. After that, I never came home if I could help it.

With my three, I tried very hard to be the kind of mother I'd wished I had. We lived in an exclusive neighborhood and the children attended prestigious schools and wore designer clothes. Not to say that things were perfect. Given Brendan's work schedule and, if I was honest, lack of real interest, most of the day to day parenting duties fell on me. But I was lucky in the sense that what Brendan denied us in time and attention, he more than made up for in cash. Brendan was one of the most successful litigators in D.C. so we wanted for nothing. Nothing material anyway. Until Veronica was in the third grade, I stayed home with the kids full time and even had the assistance of a part time nanny. So while I made sure the kids did their homework and washed behind their ears, I also cheered Mike and Timmy at all their lacrosse games and knew the ins and outs of Veronica's very intricate social life.

"You're going to hit rush hour and miss that plane if you don't get down here!"

"Oh, relax, Mom." Veronica dragged her enormous back pack down the stairs. "Our flight's not 'til six."

"Are you girls planning on hiring a sherpa to cart those things around?"

Hailey giggled. Veronica snarked, "Oh, please, Mom."

"Well, you'll build up muscle anyway. Okay, you have passports, tickets, cameras?"

"Yes, of course we do."

"All right, just checking." I handed Veronica an envelope of cash. "Make sure you tip the driver."

"I know, I know," Veronica said, in full eye roll mode.

"Come on, give your poor mother a kiss." I pulled her into an unwanted embrace. My sons were such cuddlers and still crushed me with their bear hugs but prickly Veronica was never very demonstrative and always wiggled her little body out of my frequent hugs. Well, I hopefully she'll be this averse to touch when

24

surrounded by throngs of handsome Italian men. I begged the girls to be careful as they clattered out the door.

The house was now silent, save for the distant whir of the engines of boaters lucky enough to get an early start on the weekend. I looked at my watch and saw that it was almost four. If I was lucky, I could still catch Brendan at his office before he headed off to a "client dinner" with whoever was the flavor of the month. Last I checked, it was Christine Schatten, a thirty-six year old partner in his firm's Corporate Securities department. Tall, big boned, dark-haired Christine was not his usual type. Brendan usually went for either the fresh young things in the legal assistants pool or older, elegant married women looking for a little excitement in between spa treatments and charity functions. Usually they were petite and blond, like me. But unlike me, they usually didn't last very long.

Christine with her mannish laugh and ticking biological clock? I didn't see her making it past Labor Day. We'd met over the years at various firm functions, and a few years ago had even played tennis together at the annual summer outing. Christine was always friendly, in a casual, offhand sort of way, to both myself and to Brendan. As a member of the Corporate Securities department, they didn't work together much, but then last February one of her clients was indicted for insider trading, and she brought Brendan in as defense counsel. I didn't think much of it when Brendan had to go into the office a few weekends to work with Christine, but then when I saw her at the firm's Memorial Day picnic, I knew. She'd carefully avoided looking at Brendan and when I greeted her, her voice was unnaturally high and her eyes darted around, as if looking for an escape route. I knew.

"Brendan Mills' office."

"Susan, hi. How are you?"

"I'm fine, Ellen. Thank God it's Friday, right? How are you holding up?" Susan asked, her voice full of concern. Susan had been with Brendan since he was a young associate and was looking forward to retirement next year.

"I'm hanging in there, Susan, thanks for asking. Is he in?"

"He's not in his office. I think he's down on the Corporate floor."

Of course he was. "I need to speak to him before I go back to the hospital."

"Of course, dear. Hold on." Susan had seen many Christines come and go. I knew she'd make sure he interrupted whatever he was doing and come to the phone.

"Sweetheart, how are you? I'm so glad you called." If Brendan didn't say that every time I called, in the same husky, slightly flirtatious voice, I'd almost believe him.

"Hi. Just wanted to let you know that Veronica is on her way to the airport."

"Wonderful news! I'm sure she'll have a great time."

"What's not to love about Italy, right?" I said in a pleasant, conversational voice, my default tone when discussing household matters with Brendan.

"We had a great time on our honeymoon, remember?" I recalled never ending morning sickness and Brendan flirting with the hotel maid. Yeah, good times.

"Listen," I said, wanting to end this trip down memory lane, "when do you think you'll be able to get up here?"

"I have a few cases that are really heating up. I probably won't be able to make it for at least two weeks."

"My mother may not survive two weeks, Brendan," I said, my tone no longer so pleasant.

"This insider trading case is a killer, you know that."

"And that's why you hired all those fine associates. And of course your other partners," I said, emphasizing the word partners. "Rose has been your mother-in-law for almost twenty years. She's always been fond of you, and she's been asking for you. You need to come here and at least say good-bye."

"Honey, you know if I could I would."

"I'm not asking this for me, Brendan. I'm asking for Rose. I want you here on Sunday."

"Sweetheart, be reasonable."

"Don't sweetheart me," I snapped. "Tell Christine to change whatever plans she has for you because you'll be busy saying good-bye to your dying mother-in-law." There, I'd done it. I'd broken our silent agreement never to name his current paramour.

Brendan chuckled. "You and your imagination, Ellen. You know Christine is a colleague."

"Colleague, my ass. I'm not joking here, Brendan. Do not push me on this. Sunday. By eleven. No excuses." I slammed down the phone. My heart raced as I leaned against the faded formica countertop. No matter how many times I'd had to twist Brendan's arm to participate in even the most rudimentary family activities, it never failed to rattle me. I'd had years of practice blackmailing him into attending dance recitals and graduation parties. I even had to threaten him with bodily dismemberment before he would "swing by" the hospital after Timmy's appendectomy. You would think I'd have it down by now.

I took three deep breaths, as I had learned in my many yoga classes, but of course, as usual, they didn't work. The walls of the cramped airless kitchen closed in on me. Barefoot, I rushed out of the avocado kitchen, past the ghost of the ficus in the hallway and through the front door.

A soft breeze met me as I ran down the wooden steps, and then across the road to the small boathouse. Painted a sparkling white and trimmed in the same shade of blue as the house, it sat only a few feet from the road. The pounding in my head subsided as I made my way along the narrow footpath beside the boathouse. The tiny stones pinched my bare feet. When I reached the wooden deck attached to the back of the boathouse, I lifted a wooden planter filled with cheerful red geraniums and found the boathouse key. The boathouse's new sliding glass door slid smoothly, unlike its rusted predecessor. It took a moment for my eyes to adjust to the darkness until I found the unfamiliar light switch. Last year Paul and Lisa renovated the boathouse originally built by Kitty's husband Peter, which had slowly disintegrated since Peter's death. Paul, Lisa and their children used the boathouse the most, so Lisa had gone all out, and added a small kitchenette with granite countertops, Italian terra cotta tile and a large beverage center. I helped myself to one of Lisa's bottles of pino grigio and poured a generous glass.

The deck's cushioned Adirondack chairs were a great improvement over the plastic lawn chairs of my youth. I stretched out on the one closest to the ramp that led to the small dock. The pino grigio was cold and sharp, and as I gulped my anger and tension dissipated. I stared out into the harbor and squinted in the still strong afternoon sun. I should have brought my sunglasses. The harbor was busy with several small speedboats bobbing near the bridge. Without my glasses I could just make out the rods held carelessly by the beer drinking fisherman. The men shouted over blaring 70s classic rock, surely scaring away any potential fish. In the distance a sleek gray sailboat sliced through the harbor's gentle swells and headed toward the low bridge. The boat tacked left and expertly maneuvered next to the Conroy's dock, only a few yards from my chair.

A tall sandy-haired man, early forties I'd say, shirtless and clad only in faded khaki shorts, jumped from the boat with a thick rough rope in his hand. I swallowed the remainder of my wine as he pulled the boat closer to the dock. The boat secured, he reached in and lifted out a cooler. He held the cooler in his right hand and ran his left though his wild hair. He had the hard physique of a man who clearly hadn't spend his life behind a desk. His boat was tied to our neighbor's dock so he must be one of the Conroy boys. Hard to believe this Adonis with once one of the scrappy little boys who'd hit baseballs twice through my grandmother's front window.

"Catch anything?"

He looked over and smiled. "A few fluke. Ellen, right?"

"Yes, that's right."

"Billy Conroy. " He climbed the low fence that separated the two properties and walked towards me.

"That can't be. The Billy Conroy I know had long hair and a motorcycle."

"Well," he said, "I still have the motorcycle."

"Billy, when was the last time I saw you?"

He smiled. "I think I had flunked out of college, and you were off to law school."

"It can't have been that long. Anyway, things have been so crazy I didn't have a chance to thank you. I don't know what would've happened if you hadn't found my mother when you did."

"How is she?"

"As well as can be expected, I suppose. They moved her to St. Francis Hospice last week."

Billy's bright blue eyes clouded over. "My father was at St. Francis for his last two months. It's a good place. Clean, and the staff is kind."

We were both silent for a moment and then I asked with forced cheer, "How did you manage to escape from work and go fishing?"

"Helps when you're the boss."

"I didn't realize that you owned Gold Coast Construction," I said, somehow remembering the name on the truck that was often parked in Barbara Conway's driveway.

He smiled again. "I didn't remain a screw up my whole life, Miss Murphy."

"I didn't mean it like that."

He laughed. "Yes, you did, but I'll forgive you if you pour me a glass of that wine."

"Of course, sit down and I'll get you a glass." Billy took the chair next to mine. In Lisa's well stocked kitchen, I loaded a tray with the bottle of pino, a glass for Billy, a small bowl of salsa and large bowl of nachos.

"I brought a few snacks." I set the tray down on a side table.

"Perfect."

After I filled the glasses, I sank into my chair. "When did you become such a sailor? Didn't you used to avoid your dad's sailboat like the plague?"

He laughed. "Probably because he wouldn't let me smoke pot on it. No, the boat was my dad's and Jimmy's thing. And Tom's when he wasn't busy memorizing the periodic table."

"It must be tough being the black sheep. What have your brothers been up to anyway?"

"Jimmy's a hot shot lawyer in the city and Tom's an oncologist out in California. They're both married, Jimmy has three kids and Tom has four."

"Impressive. Barbara must be proud."

"Yeah, although who does she call when she needs a bulb changed or the driveway shoveled? Yours truly." Billy smiled, but was unable to hide the sting underneath.

"You have your own business, Billy. She must be proud of you too."

"Yeah, well, you'd have to ask her."

"So you never answered my question. When did you start sailing?"

"I'd say about fifteen years ago. My father was so happy that I was finally interested, and once Jimmy wasn't around to tell me what I was doing wrong, I enjoyed it. Almost up until the end, my father loved going out with me and Kyle, so I was glad that I had taken it up."

"Kyle?"

"My son. He's fourteen."

"I didn't know you were married." Billy, with his ripped muscles and wild hair, didn't give off a married vibe.

"Divorced. Melanie lives with her new husband in Cold Spring Harbor. He's a dentist. Kyle splits his time between there and my house in Northport."

"A dentist?" I could not imagine leaving a hunk like Billy to marry some nerdy dentist.

As if reading my thoughts, Billy said, "I know, but the truth is I wasn't the best husband. I worked construction sporadically. Spent a lot of my time on my bike and with my friends. Probably too much time at Gunther's bar. Melanie liked to pretend she was a bad girl, but once we had Kyle that changed. She lost patience with me, I guess. But now we're friends. Melanie leaving me was probably the best thing that could've happened. After that, I settled down, borrowed some money from my dad, and started my company."

"Well, it sounds like everything worked out."

"It has, I guess. What about you. You still married?"

"Yes. My husband's a partner at a law firm in D.C. He talks about retirement, but I'll believe it when I see it. They'll have to pry the blackberry from his cold dead hands."

"Oh, that's right. My mom told me that you married an old dude."

I laughed. "If Brendan could hear you calling him an old dude, he would die. He thinks he's sixty going on twenty-six."

"He's sixty? But wait, you're only a year or two older than me, right?"

"That's right. I'm forty-three. But believe me, his age is the least of our problems."

"I'm sorry to hear that."

God, I didn't mean to say that. I sputtered, "I mean with my mother and all."

"Of course. How is she, really?" Billy placed his strong warm hand on mine. I shivered slightly; it had been an eternity since a man had touched me.

"We're getting near the end now."

We were both silent then, his hand remained on mine while we looked out onto the water. I felt the band of tension lodged across my shoulder loosen.

Billy took his hand off mine. "Listen, Ellen, I have all this fish and no one to share it with me. Why don't you let me cook you dinner?"

"I would love that, Billy." I looked at my watch. "But, I should've been at St. Francis an hour ago. I promised to relieve my uncle Danny by five, and its almost six now. Can I take a rain check?"

"Of course, any time."

I awkwardly stood up and Billy grabbed the tray and took it into the boathouse. Before I could stop him, he had rinsed out the glasses and put the tray away. I couldn't remember the last time Brendan put his coffee cup in the dishwasher.

We walked out of the boathouse in silence, and I locked the door and lifted the planter to return the key. I then turned to him. "Thanks for sitting with me. It really helped me take my mind off things."

Without warning, Billy took me into his arms and gave me a hug. He smelled of saltwater. My pulse quickened as his strong arms surrounded me. "Ellen, I know this is a terrible time," he said into my ear. He then released me. "It's easy to get caught up caring for the sick person. You have to remember to take care of yourself as well."

I willed my cheeks not to blush, to no avail. Jesus, I thought, I'm a grown woman, not a horny teenager. I forced myself to adopt a friendly, but detached tone. "I will. Thanks again. I'll see you around."

Billy gave me a little wave as he headed back to the boat.

Chapter 5

Rose

I sat up, looked around the unfamiliar room and missed, for not the first time, the heavy rhythmic breathing of my cousin Molly. I wriggled out of the tight sheets and swung my feet over the side of the high narrow bed. The floor was cold and I shivered in my thin nightdress. I crept to the door and opened it, slowly, and prayed it wouldn't creak. The hallway was dark except for a faint line of light underneath my mother's door. All was quiet except for the clang of a distant buoy.

I turned to go back to bed when a low thumping sound stopped me. I walked into the hallway and placed my hand on the door to my mother's room. The door vibrated as if something was being thrown against it. I turned the brass doorknob and pushed against the door with all my might.

"Go back to bed!" my mother shouted. A stream of blood dripped from her forehead.

"Mama! Mama what's wrong?"

Her voice ragged with tears, she said, "Rosie, love, go to bed."

"No, Mama."

Peter came up behind her, threw open the door and pushed Mama to the floor. In the light I could see her left eye was swollen and almost completely shut. I stepped back and fell against the hallway table. A porcelain vase crashed to the floor. "Sorry, Peter," I whimpered. "I'm sorry."

Peter lifted me like a rag doll and threw me onto my bed. My head slammed against the wooden headboard. Then darkness.

* * *

Ellen

I looked in the rearview mirror. My roots were over an inch long. Back home, every four weeks I religiously visited the same Georgetown salon frequented by the First Lady. I'd forgotten that under my carefully maintained artifice of "number 5, ash blonde" lay the same steel grey strands that covered my mother's head. How could I've thought that hot Billy Conroy was flirting with me? No man would look at me twice in this state. "Ellen, grab hold of yourself," I muttered. It's not like I'd ever given Billy or his scrawny overachieving brothers the time of day in high school.

I walked through the now familiar halls of St. Francis and tried to shake off all thoughts of Billy and my seemingly awakened libido. Armed with a large thermos of coffee and a stack of magazines, I braced myself for the evening shift. The door to my mother's room was ajar. She was asleep while my uncle Danny read in the corner.

"Sorry I'm late, Danny," I whispered.

Danny looked up, his wire rim glasses perched on his large nose. "No problem. You okay?"

I ran my fingers through my lank two-toned hair. "Yeah, just a little tired."

"I can stay tonight if you want to go home and get some rest." Danny's long thin face was pale, as though it was January and not July. I wasn't the only one suffering through the ordeal of Rose's illness.

"No, I'll be fine. I'm a bit drained, that's all."

"You've been great, Ellen. I know it wasn't easy for you to drop everything and come up here, what with your big job and all. But we appreciate it. Me, Paul, Molly."

I smiled. "Maybe not Molly."

"No, even Molly. She knows how much your being here means to your mother."

"To tell you the truth, sometimes I feel like I do more harm than good. Either Mom's so out of it from the drugs that she doesn't know I'm here or when she is awake, I snap at her and say the wrong thing."

Danny shook his head. "No, I'm sure that's not true."

"It is, Danny. We haven't been close for years. Hell, I don't think we were ever close. And now, well, now it's too late to do much about it."

"Ellen, you were her life. You have to know that."

"I don't think I know anything anymore."

"You have to stop beating yourself up," Danny said, his homely face filled with concern. "It won't help Rose and it won't help you."

33

"You're right. I know you're right." I leaned against a table and knocked over a vase. The vase fell and shattered.

"I'm such an idiot." I crouched down to pick up pieces of the cheap glass.

"It's fine, it's fine. There are too many damn flowers in here anyway. I'll get the paper towels." Danny walked to the bathroom.

"Mama!" Rose shouted from the bed.

My mother sat up, her eyes wide with fear.

"Mom? What is it?"

"Mama, Mama open the door!" Rose said, her voice high and trembling.

"It's me, Mom. It's Ellen. You're okay, everything's okay."

Danny walked over from the bathroom and grabbed Rose's hand. "Rose? Rose, are you all right?"

Rose stared at Danny and howled like a wounded animal. Danny and I looked at each other, frozen. Neither of us knew what to do.

My mother said in a small, pitiful voice, "Peter, I'm sorry. I didn't mean to break it. I'm sorry Peter, don't hurt me."

I looked at kind, sweet Danny who unfortunately bore an uncanny resemblance to his father. "Danny, go get the nurse."

Rose took my hand and repeated, in a frantic shriek, "Mama, Mama, Mama."

Almost instantly I channeled my grandmother, and said, "Rosie, love, you're all right. Hush pet, everything's fine." I rubbed her back, as I would a small child. "Ah, Rosie, you're my girl, you're my good girl." My mother smiled at me, uncertainly. "That's right, Rosie, lie back."

I slowly stroked my mother's hair, and murmured what I could remember of Kitty's comforting phrases. The nurse inserted a needle in her arm while Danny looked on. After a few moments, Rose's face went slack.

"She should sleep through the night now," the stout nurse said.

"She was so confused. What caused that? Was it her medication?" I asked.

"They get like that near the end." The nurse shrugged, although her broad face was sympathetic.

I turned to Danny. "Have you seen her like that before? I know she's been in pain and out of it sometimes, but never like this."

"I guess it's just what the nurse said. She's near the end."

"But they said she had another few weeks," my voice rose an octave.

"They said she could have another few weeks, Ellen," Danny said.

I sank onto the chair next to her bed. "It's too soon. I'm not ready."

Chapter 6

Ellen

"Laurie, you're a miracle worker."

"You like it? I wasn't sure you were in the right frame of mind for something so radical."

I ran my fingers along my now naked neck. Long strands of blonde hair carpeting the salon's bleached oak floor. Laurie, wearing the same quizzical expression she'd always had in algebra class, stood behind me.

I looked at Laurie in the mirror. "I love it. Honestly, I do. Especially the color."

"Yeah, you needed to tone it down. It was getting a little brassy."

I laughed. "I'll be sure to tell that to my overpriced salon in D.C. But really Laurie, thanks. I feel like a new woman."

"Who says Centerport doesn't have style." My old high school pal's hands swept the small yet sleek salon she'd opened after her painful divorce. "Hey, you wanna grab some lunch? My next appointment's not 'til one."

"I would love to, but I need to get over to St. Francis. My mother had a rough night last night."

"Of course, sweetie. But listen, keep me updated. Don't just sneak off to D.C. without letting me know, okay?"

"I will. I promise."

I crossed the parking lot to Frohller's Hardware. Danny had recently painted the clapboard siding a dull green, but other than that, not much had changed from the days Kitty sold her homemade soda bread alongside hammers and nails. The ancient floorboards creaked as I made my way up the cluttered aisle. Carol, Danny's wife, sat beside the cash register, and patiently explained the difference between two screwdrivers to an elderly woman. I hung back until she was finished.

"Oh my God, Ellen. I almost didn't recognize you!"

"I needed a change. Laurie Nolan did it. Do you like it?"

"I love it! Maybe I should have her do something with this." Carol grabbed a handful of her over permed hair. Like a lot of women, especially women on Long Island, Carol was very attached to her big hair.

"Sure," I said diplomatically, although I doubted Carol would ever update her '80s do, despite the fact that she was fast approaching fifty. "Danny around?"

"He's in the back, doing inventory. Listen, Ellie, I'm glad you're here. Could I ask you a favor?"

"Of course."

"It's our fifth wedding anniversary tomorrow and I made reservations at Pablo's for dinner. I know Danny is supposed to sit with your mother tonight, but would you mind switching with him? I can go stay with your mother this afternoon if you could go this evening."

I couldn't remember the last time Brendan even acknowledged our anniversary. I looked at Carol with her big hair and big smile and tried not to be jealous of the obviously close bond she had with my uncle. We were all surprised when Danny, never much of a lady killer, announced at age fifty-three that he was getting married. We were even more surprised when he showed up with the bubbly Carol. But shy Danny simply adored her and it looked like five years in, they were still going strong.

"If you could go this afternoon that would be great. Doing the day and evening shift can be a bit much," I said. "Plus, I should probably do something about the front lawn before Lisa has a fit."

"Don't let Lisa get to you. I never do. You should go home and relax."

I took Carol's advice and passed by the overgrown grass without too much guilt. I went into the kitchen and made myself a chicken salad sandwich. While I ate at the small kitchen table, I opened my laptop and scrolled through emails. There were a few emails from work, although fewer than I'd expected. It appeared that the U.S. government was able to roll along without my presence. My son Timmy sent a funny email updating me on the latest scandal at the Virginia country club where he was a lifeguard for the summer. Veronica checked in with an airy email that conveyed absolutely no information—she could have spent the week shopping in the local mall for all I could tell from her missive. I hoped that for $40,000 a year, NYU improves her writing style.

I swallowed the last of my iced tea and then walked to the dryer in the corner and pulled out a pair of sheets. I hadn't heard from Brendan since our call yesterday, so I'd assumed that he would make an appearance tomorrow. If he knew what was good for him, he would. Since I was sleeping in my old bedroom, the boys' bedroom was filled to the ceiling with boxes and it didn't seem right to put him in my mother's bedroom, I needed to prepare Kitty's room for my wayward husband.

I climbed the stairs with the freshly laundered sheets. Dust had settled in the grooves of the banister. Maybe I'd have time to run the vacuum around in the morning before Brendan arrived; he hated a messy house. The door to Kitty's room opened with a slow squeak. The room was hot. I opened the windows and allowed the rank air of low tide to fill the room. I pulled the heavy down comforter off the sheet-less bed with a vigorous tug and replaced it with clean sheets and a light lace quilt I'd found in the hall closet.

That done, I gathered the various remnants of the room's prior occupant: hairpins, a pair of glasses, a sticky half empty bottle of cough medicine. After I tossed the detritus in a half filled wastepaper basket, I approached the old chest of drawers. The top drawer held only a few lace handkerchiefs and a ripped pair of stocking, so I threw them in the basket as well. Now at least Brendan would have someplace to put his underwear and socks. I opened the closet to find it still empty after my purge five years earlier. Good. Now he would have somewhere to hang his expensive suits.

I went downstairs for another glass of iced tea, furniture polish and a handful of rags. I rubbed the polish along the bed's headboard and the side tables. The strong smell of lemon masked the bedroom's stale air.

When I was done, I sat down on the bed and sipped iced tea. I scanned the room. Brendan wouldn't like sleeping here, but it'll only be for a few days, and hopefully he'll be smart enough not to complain.

I looked around the room one last time to see if anything else was out of order. The two bottom drawers of the old chest were still ajar from my digging expedition the previous week. I walked over to the chest and crouched down to push the drawers closed, but both were stuck. I opened the bottom drawer and arranged the stack of envelopes so they laid flat, but the drawer still wouldn't close. In exasperation, I pulled open the drawer and dumped the contents onto the floor.

I sorted through the old letters. Curious, I opened a few. Most were from my great-grandmother, Eileen O'Connor, and included reports to Kitty of the activities of the farm: the birth of a new calf, how much hay was cut, and hopes that the rain would hold off until it had been brought in. It seems nine times out of ten, the weather didn't hold. They were in rainy Ireland, I thought, how could they have been surprised? Eileen also kept Kitty up to date on her younger siblings' activities and the local gossip. I'd obviously never met my namesake, but through these simple notes I got a sense of her strength and her pious nature.

What must it have been like for her to give birth to nine children, see two die and four others be lost to her through immigration? She wrote often to her eldest daughter, at a time when she likely could spare neither the time nor the few pennies for paper and postage. Eileen must have wanted to keep Kitty close to her, tied to Templeglantin, in spirit if not in body.

It appeared that she was successful, at least initially, because Kitty wrote back cheery letters to her family in Templeglantin, and always asked detailed questions about each member. In one of her early letters, she was excited to hear that her sister Margaret would be joining her, although she warned her not to expect America to be the paradise that their neighbors, the Sheehans, had portrayed it to be.

It was only after Margaret arrived in New York that the tone of Eileen's letters changed. Apparently Kitty had been selective in what she told her mother. Eileen believed that Kitty worked in a parish rectory, which was the job that Bridie Sheehan's daughter had arranged for her. The truth was, as Margaret must have told her mother, Kitty didn't last two weeks scrubbing for the cranky old pastor and his exacting young assistant. Instead, she found a job at Flannery's on Second Avenue in Manhattan, making sandwiches and serving drinks when the pub was busy. *"I make twice what Father Healy paid me, for half the effort,"* Kitty wrote in her schoolgirl scrawl. *"Now I can send you more money to pay for Maura's passage,"* Maura was next in line for the immigrant ship. Eileen may have accepted Kitty's ill gotten gains, but that didn't mean that she didn't lecture her about looking for a *"more suitable position."*

The letters took on a more cheerful tone a few months later as they discussed Margaret's upcoming wedding. *"My heart is pure broke that I have to miss Margaret's big day, but I know, dear girl, that you will do the family proud and stand in for us."* She went on to comfort Kitty, who being three years older than Margaret, was still unmarried. *"Pray to God daughter, that he may send you as fine as man as He found for your sister. Do not lose heart, dear child, for God is good."*

A few months later, Eileen's heart was truly broken when she heard of Kitty's betrayal of her sister. *"I have walked the house these three nights, unable to sleep after hearing your sorry news from Bridie Sheehan. All of Kilvarren village and all of Brooklyn must know your shameful story. I cannot show my face in town, and your poor father is destroyed. But I will not talk of your sins, daughter, for the time to talk has passed. Margaret writes that you are to be wed. Hopefully God in His infinite mercy may bless this union and bless your child. That is what I pray for each and every night. Your good sister has agreed to stand with you. I pray that God gives her the strength to get through what for her will be a hard day. To see you in her dress, and she wearing yours, will be difficult, but I know Our Father will reward her soon, for not shaming her family and for being a good sister to you. A better sister than you deserve. But we will speak of that no more. Be sure to send pictures, so that we can show the Sheehans and our other neighbors. God Bless."*

Eileen must have gotten her picture, but there were no more letters in the drawer from her until Tim Murphy's death, although there were many persistently cheerful letters from Kitty addressed to Eileen during that time, letters extolling the beauty of her daughter Rose and the good nature of her handsome husband. She described for Eileen every stick of furniture in her new basement apartment in Park Slope, every dress she knitted for Rose, but apparently received nothing in return. Kitty determinedly continued to write, as if responding to her mother's letters as before. Then the letters from Kitty stopped, and a month after my grandfather's death, Eileen wrote:

"My dear darling Kitty, My heart is broken writing this letter to you, also your father and your brothers and sisters. I nearly dropped dead myself when I read that your poor loving husband was dead. What a shock it was to us and what it must be to you. May God and His Blessed Mother comfort you and your child. May God rest his poor soul.

Oh Kitty dear, I beg you not to worry yourself to death. You have something to live for, your child. She will need you and she will cheer you. I am not able to write, my head and my heart is paining me so. Kitty, if you want to come home there is a place here for you and your child. Our hearts are open to receive you and comfort you for as long as we live. If you stay in that sad land, I am sure your good sisters will help you and your child. The past is over, dear child, and we must all remember that we are all the one.

Kitty dear, I can write no more. My eyes are blind with tears. Write to me soon. I will be worrying until I hear from you."

My own eyes were blind with tears when I finished that letter, but I couldn't help myself, I continued on and read about how Kitty had to leave her beloved basement apartment to take a nursing job in Manhattan, leaving her small child with her sister. But in time, Kitty did cheer up, perhaps too much to suit her mother for in her letters she scolded Kitty for not sending Margaret enough support money, not visiting Rose often enough and, according to Mrs. Sheehan and her omnipotent relations, consorting with a *"bad element."*

She sent Kitty a blistering letter when she learned that she intended to take Rose from Margaret. *"Surely, my bold daughter, you are speaking out of temper and not from sense. If Rose calls your sister mother, it's because she doesn't see enough of you. Your good sister is not to blame. Where would you be without her generous heart? Look where your jealousy and spite got you last time. Apologize to your sister and her fine husband, visit your daughter every week, and stop this nonsense about marrying that quare fellow that Margaret says you brought to the house last week. I will pray that Our Blessed Mother guides you and gives you strength."*

The next letter was more conciliatory and almost pleading. *"Margaret tells me that you are to be wed next month. I pray that he is a fine man and that he will take care of you and Rosie. But how do you know this man? Who is his family and why does he live so far from Brooklyn and your sisters? I pray to our Lord in Heaven that you find happiness in this marriage, if you do marry him. But please know that your child is happy and loved in Margaret's home. The thought of losing her is breaking your sister's heart. Maybe it would be best not to move the child. I pray to God that all turns out well."*

Well, Kitty did marry her quare fellow and take back her child. For about a year, their correspondence was frequent. Kitty described her new home by the sea and the customers in the village hardware shop that her husband's family owned while Eileen described the details of her husband's wake and funeral and her son Danny's subsequent marriage to a Sheehan. If mother and daughter were not as close as they once were, they were closer than they had been since Kitty's ill fated marriage to Tim Murphy. But then Eileen sent this letter: *"My Dear Kitty, I am holding Margaret's letter in my hand and I can't believe it. She says that when she saw you last, she was shocked by your condition.. She said that your pretty hair is thin, and even missing in places and that the child is in even worse shape with bruises on her arm and a scar on her neck. Dear child, what is happening? You must tell me. Do not let pride stop you from seeking help. Sure, isn't Margaret's John a police sergeant? Let him help you. Your brother Danny says to tell you that there is always a place for you here. Even his wife Maggie agrees, and well, despite her being a Sheehan, she's not the worst of them. We would make room for you and your dear child. Please God, you are safe and I will wait for your next letter."*

Kitty's response was short and savage. *"If my sister cannot visit without carrying tales, then's she's no longer welcome in my home, and you can tell her that. I'm fine and my child is fine, and for that one to say otherwise and cause trouble, well I won't stand for it. Rose is an active child and gets into everything, so of course she gets bruises. I know my hair has thinned, but it's from the pregnancy. Does Margaret honestly believe my husband would pull my hair? Peter is a good and kind husband and I will not hear anything against him. You can tell my brother and the Sheehans that all is well for us on Long Island."*

I put down the letter, the thin paper almost transparent with age. The breeze from the window was now cool and the sun was low. I dropped the letters and hurried out of the room so as not to be late.

I made it to my mother's room at St. Francis by seven, to the obvious relief of Carol.

"How is she?" I asked.

"More alert today, for a little while anyway. She finished her dinner and drifted off about a half hour ago." Carol picked up a purse the size of a suitcase.

"She wasn't upset or anything?"

"No, El, she was just her usual sweet self. Listen, hon, I really gotta go before we lose that reservation."

"Of course, go on. Have a good time."

With a quick wave, she was off. I turned to my mother, whose color was a little better. Her sleep seemed untroubled by the dreams that disturbed her yesterday.

If that's what they were. What if they were memories? What did she say yesterday—don't hurt me, Peter? I tried to recall whether there had been any hint from my mother or Kitty that Peter was a little quick with his hands. But there was nothing. They never spoke about Peter. Other than the stiff family portrait taken at Danny's baptism, there were no pictures of Peter that I remembered even seeing at home, and that lone picture soon disappeared after Kitty's funeral. Besides the fact that he left two sons, it was as if the man had never lived.

But wasn't that in itself a sign? I grew up in what was essentially that man's house—it had been in the Frohller family since it was built in 1886—and I knew next to nothing about Peter Frohller. Didn't that speak volumes?

I couldn't imagine anyone less likely to be a battered wife than Kitty. Kitty, who buried two husbands by age forty-three and raised three children and a grandchild, was the most capable woman I'd ever met. I could still see her with her hand on her hip as she harangued a poor delivery man who delivered the wrong size nails. Someone hit bold Kitty? How could they dare?

But a woman of sixty, safe and secure in her own home and with money in the bank was a far cry from a young immigrant of twenty-five with a young child to care for. Would she suffer in silence just to give her child a home? I didn't know the answer to that. I'd never met a scared and vulnerable Kitty.

Maybe Margaret got it wrong. Maybe my mother was just an active and somewhat clumsy child. My son Timmy was one big

43

bruise from ages three to six. Surely Kitty wouldn't subject her own child to the violence described in that letter because she didn't want to admit to her family that she had been wrong to marry Peter. I had put up with a lot from my own husband, maybe too much, but he'd soon find himself in the trunk of his precious sedan if he hurt one of our children. Surely Kitty would've felt the same.

My mother stirred in the bed. With all the weight loss, her features were sharper than ever, but what was heartbreaking when she was awake was almost child-like in sleep. Did Peter hurt her? Was that why she was so meek and mild, because Peter had beaten the spirit out of her? I didn't know what upset me more, the thought of someone harming a small defenseless Rose or the fact that I had no clue as to who the woman lying on the bed really was.

The letter said Rose had a scar on her neck. My mother didn't have a scar, did she? If there was no scar, then maybe Margaret's letter to Eileen and her letter to Kitty were just a misunderstanding, a Bay Ridge to Templeglantin to Centerport game of telephone that had gone horribly wrong. If there was no scar, then maybe there was no abuse.

I bent closer to my mother and examined her neck. Just as I thought, there was no scar. Relief washed over me as I sat back in my chair. "I'm overwrought," I thought, "and I have no business going through Rose's and Kitty's things." Molly was right, I should leave those musty letters alone. I had upset myself over nothing.

I walked down to the vending machine on the first floor and bought myself a cup of weak coffee. I chatted briefly to one of the night nurses who handed me the most recent celebrity magazine. I promised to give her my newspaper when I was finished with it. In a much better frame of mind, I returned to my mother's room, and proceeded to read through the trashy mags.

About an hour and a half later, one of the aides stuck her head in the door. "Mrs. Mills? It's almost eleven. Visiting hours are over."

"Yes, of course. I lost track of time." I put down the magazine and looked at my mother who had turned on her side, faced away from me, while I had been engrossed by the latest celebrity dust-up. The back of her thin neck was fully exposed. In the soft light, I could see a mark that almost looked as if it had been made from the sheets. I moved closer until I saw it: a jagged silvery line that reached halfway down my mother's neck.

44

Chapter 7

Ellen

By ten o'clock, I was up, dressed and fit to be tied. No sign of Brendan, no call to tell me he'd be late. Well, I'd cut my fingers off before I dialed him.

I rearranged the plate of bagels I'd rushed out to buy this morning and then walked into the hallway and fussed with the arrangement of flowers I'd cut from the garden earlier. I looked into the hallway's old brass mirror and ran my hands through my newly shorn hair.

Back in the kitchen, I poured myself a mug of coffee. I didn't want to be found by Brendan waiting on the steps, like a child waiting for Santa, so I took a new magazine and my coffee to the back patio. I sat on the flimsy lawn chair and attempted to focus on the lush flowers while ignoring the equally abundant weeds.

I looked at the heavy platinum and diamond Cartier watch the children guilted Brendan into buying me for my 40th birthday. Twenty-five to eleven. I fought the urge to call him and focused instead on the latest celebutantes and their various weight loss tricks.

Two minutes later, a car door slammed followed by the faint chime of the doorbell. I forced myself to walk slowly into the house, through the kitchen and the hallway to the heavy oak front door. "Brendan," I said, feigning slight disinterest, "you made it."

"Of course, sweetheart." He swept me into a hearty embrace. "I said I would be here."

I disentangled myself from his arms. "So you did. Why don't you drop your bag in the living room and we'll be off."

"What, no coffee?" Brendan barreled into the kitchen. His large frame overwhelmed the small room. "Ooo, bagels."

I followed him. "We don't have time."

"Sure we do, hon, she's not going anywhere."

I poured him a cup of coffee. "Nice, Brendan."

"Aw, that's not what I meant. I just drove six hours through horrendous New York traffic. Cut me some slack, boss."

I sighed. "Do you want cream cheese?"

"Of course! Load me up."

After Brendan was fed and watered, we walked to my car, where I received a wave from a shirtless and sweaty Billy. For some reason this piqued Brendan's interest. "You're friendly with the gardener, honey?"

"That's the neighbor's son. We went to high school together."

"I'll bet he had a huge crush on you."

"We didn't exactly run in the same circles."

"I'm sure all the boys loved you," Brendan said with his usual flirty smile.

I didn't even bother to answer. I turned up the radio and neither of us spoke again during our ride to St. Francis. Once there, we walked past the nurses at the front desk who gave me a smile and Brendan an appraising look. At fifty-nine, Brendan, with his broad shoulders, deep set blue-grey eyes and thick mane of silver hair, still cut an impressive figure. We had almost reached my mother's room, when he touched my hair. "Hey, did you do something to your hair?"

"Yeah, I cut off six inches." And it only took you an hour to notice, I sniped in my head.

"Lookin' good, kid," he said with the same smile he'd give his secretary Susan if she bought a new pair of glasses.

I stifled my irritation and said thank you as we walked into my mother's room. My mother looked anxious as her friend from her convent days, Sister Elizabeth, read from the bible. Sister Elizabeth stopped reading and beamed at us.

"Well, here they are now, Rose. I told you they'd be along soon."

"Sorry we're late," I said.

"Not at all. It gave me a chance to catch up with Rose. I was out last week at a retreat." The small wren-like woman rose quickly and gave Brendan her seat. "Now, I'll leave you alone to enjoy your visit."

"Bye, Elizabeth," my mother said faintly.

"Good-bye, Sister Elizabeth," I said.

Sister smiled. "See you later. I'll stop in before I leave."

Even sitting, Brendan's large frame overwhelmed the small room. In a booming voice he said, "So, look at my favorite mother-in-law. Are they treating you okay?"

"Oh, yes, Brendan." Rose struggled to sit up. I ran to the other side of her bed and propped a pillow behind her back.

"And you're not causing any trouble here? Have the male nurses fallen in love with you yet, Rose?"

Unbelievably, my mother always loved Brendan's ridiculous banter, the more hokey, the better.

"Oh, Brendan, you're terrible." Her small thin hand playfully tapped his. They went on like that for another twenty minutes until Rose's energy flagged. She must have felt herself go, because she took Brendan's hand. "Brendan, thank you for taking such good care of my Ellen all these years. I knew the first time I met you, that you were a good man and that you'd make my daughter happy."

"I'm the lucky one, Rose. Lucky to have two such beautiful women in my life," Brendan said, a typical glib response.

"No, Brendan," she said, her voice no louder than a whisper now, "I'm serious. You gave Ellen a real home and family, something I couldn't do. For that I've always been grateful. May God bless you and keep you." Tears welled in her eyes, and Brendan looked at me, slightly panicked. Brendan could never handle real emotions. I saved him and said, "Mom, Brendan has always told me how you were a second mother to him." I poked him, hard. "Didn't you, dear?"

"Oh yes, Rose. I always say that."

My mother nodded. Her lids fluttered as she fought the fatigue. Within minutes, she succumbed.

Brendan slapped his hands on his knees. "Well, what now?"

"What do you mean, what now?" I snapped. "We wait until she wakes up."

He looked slightly confused. "But I said good-bye. Isn't that what you wanted?"

"Paul will be here at four to start the night shift. We'll stay until then."

"Is it really necessary for one of you to just sit here all day?" Brendan asked, unable to hide his exasperation. "Isn't that what the nurses are for?"

"Brendan, she's dying. In a matter of a few weeks, maybe just a few more days for all the doctors know. I'm not going to let her die alone. I can't believe I really have to spell it out for you."

"Fine, fine. No need to get upset."

"My mother's dying and you're acting like a total shit. If anyone has a right to get upset it's me. Why don't you go outside and make whatever calls you need to make. She should be asleep for a while."

He brightened. "Okay, but only if you're sure."

"Just go, Brendan."

I flipped through an old paperback, although it was difficult to concentrate. After a while, I gave up and walked over to the window. Brendan paced along the courtyard and shouted into his cell. Either his insider trading case wasn't going well or Christine was giving him an earful for disrupting their weekend plans. The older woman kneeling at the statue of Mary shot Brendan disapproving looks which I doubt he even noticed. The woman eventually gave up and left.

As I looked at Brendan from this distance, I tried to remember what it was that originally entranced me so. To be honest, I'd never had a shortage of boyfriends, and while Brendan with his dark auburn hair and brash confidence was certainly attractive, he wasn't the best looking guy I'd ever dated. I certainly didn't think of him as boyfriend material when he first interviewed me for a summer associate position at his white shoe law firm. To me, he was yet another middle-aged partner I had to try and impress with my middling law school grades. Not surprisingly, his firm didn't give me an offer since they usually limited their summer associate class to the brainiacs on law review. What was surprising was the phone message he left me three weeks later.

My dates in law school usually consisted of keg parties at dingy Capital Hill apartments or if a guy was really trying to impress me, a burger and pitcher at a nearby dank Irish pub. Brendan took me to only the finest restaurants, sprinkled with tickets to the Kennedy Center. As an impoverished student subsisting on meager student loans, initially the meals were as much of an attraction as the man. However, Brendan slowly won me over. When he turned on the charm, you really felt like the most beautiful, most intriguing woman in the world, and such concentrated attention was intoxicating. And the sex, well it was intoxicating as well, especially since it occurred in his elegant Georgetown townhouse rather than a cramped student share house that smelt of dirty socks and cheap aftershave. Although I had to laugh when on our first night together after Brendan disentangled himself from my naked limbs, he scampered quickly to the bathroom and returned wearing a robe, striped pajamas and slippers. I told him he looked like an old man. Little did I know then I'd spend the next twenty years washing and ironing replicas of those ridiculous pajamas.

It was only after we had been together six months that I began to suspect that I wasn't the only girl on Brendan's dance card. Oh, I'd say I was the primary girlfriend. After all, I attended his firm functions and he introduced me to his parents, but there were a few signs: the message a girl with a sultry Southern accent left on his answering machine while he was in the shower, the Friday nights when he worked "late."

I wondered now, what would've happened if I had confronted him about it. Would he have denied it? Would he have sworn to change his ways, begged me not to leave him? Well, I'd never know because I never said a word. I continued to spend three or four nights a week with him in Georgetown, attended his nephew's christening, and played the part of the happy girlfriend. And a few months later when I was pregnant, with twins no less, I played the part of the happy fiancé and then the happy wife and mother.

How long he was faithful to me? After the boys were born I was enveloped by the fog of motherhood and didn't have the energy to keep a close eye on him. Even so, in the early years Brendan made an effort. He was home most weekends, was generally attentive, and we still had an amazing sex life. But, honestly, I didn't look too closely. I accepted things at face value, and when he claimed to be working late, I made myself believe he was working late. And when he lingered too long in a corner at a neighbor's barbecue talking to someone's younger sister, I accepted his explanation that he was just being friendly.

I probably would've stayed in my bubble of denial had it not been for Kitty. Rose and Kitty came down to D.C. for Veronica's Holy Communion party. Brendan was in a corner laughing with Nancy Shanley, my Bunco friend, when Kitty took me aside.

"Now that your young lady is in school, you could surely get a job," Kitty stated rather than asked.

"I'm really busy with the kids, Gran. Besides Brendan makes plenty of money. It really wouldn't be worth it for me to work part time."

She looked over at Brendan. "Do what you want, but if it was me, I'd get something of my own. Just in case."

My canny grandmother had seen in a few moments what I had blinded myself to for a decade. I didn't know why that conversation made such an impact on me, but after that the blinders were off. I kept track of Brendan's comings and goings, scoured through his credit card bills, even followed him to a hotel in the company of a petite young blonde. It was so easy. He didn't even attempt to hide it from me. Soon after that, I got a job at the SEC. Our sex life together eventually petered out, and when the kids were in high school, I moved Brendan into the guest room.

I turned from the window and returned to my seat by the bed. My mother's breathing in the last few days had turned ragged. Sister Elizabeth told me that this was to be expected; as they got closer to the end, many developed what the nurses called the death rattle. With a shudder, I read my book. About an hour later, Brendan returned with two coffees and a newspaper.

"Before you ask, we have another two hours until Paul gets here," I growled without even looking up from my book.

"Who's asking? You want the main section or metro?" Brendan handed me the coffee.

"The style section. I can't deal with the real world just yet."

"Whatever you say, boss." He tossed me the paper and then settled into the chair closest to the window. For the next two hours, we wordlessly passed sections of the paper back and forth as Rose slept.

Later, Lisa bustled into the room with an enormous bouquet of cheap carnations. "Brendan, I didn't expect to see you here." Lisa panted slightly as she placed the flowers on the side table.

"Brendan came up for a few days. Lisa, how did you know that carnations are my mother's favorite flower?" I asked sweetly. Rose detested carnations.

"I think she mentioned it once."

"Well, they are beautiful," Brendan said in an attempt to diffuse the situation. Brendan didn't know much about my inner life, but even he knew how much I couldn't stand Lisa.

"How was the wedding?" I asked.

"Well, your uncle had too good a time, so he's back at the house trying to recover," Lisa said in full martyr mode.

Brendan stood up. "We haven't eaten, so if you don't mind, Lisa, we'll be off."

I had wanted to wait until my mother woke up again, but the thought of being trapped in a room with Brendan, Lisa and those obnoxious carnations was not appealing. "Sure. Let's go."

"Where to now?" Brendan asked when we drove out of the parking lot.

"Home."

"Sorry, El, but I'm not up for going back to that house. Why don't we go to the place on the water you took me to last time?"

"Prime?"

"Yeah, let's go there."

"It's only four. Isn't it a little early for steak?"

"Sweetheart, it's never too early for steak."

Suddenly, I was starving. I hadn't eaten much more than the occasional sandwich during the last few weeks. The restaurant wasn't open yet for dinner. Brendan slipped the hostess a twenty. She led us to an outdoor patio and brought us two strong martinis. I didn't have the energy or the interest to respond to Brendan's banalities so after a while he stopped talking, and we sat there quietly and drank our martinis while the boats sailed by.

By the second martini, the restaurant opened and the waiter bought us two T-Bones, which we ate in silence, although the silence was now companionable rather than strained. By dessert and my third martini, I was feeling a bit "merry" as my grandmother would say, and was ready to talk to Brendan. Grateful for a now appreciative audience, Brendan regaled me with his latest office coup, one of his many attempts to displace his law firm's current managing partner.

We chatted about country club gossip and our sons' complicated love lives during martini number four. I laughed at Brendan's flirty banter; he was a philandering asshole, but he could be very funny, especially after a few drinks. It was still light out when I swayed through the restaurant parking lot to my car. Brendan, who was sober, at least compared to me, drove us home.

He helped me out of the car and up the steep front steps.

"Good evening, Ellen," Barbara Conroy trilled from her front porch.

"Hi, Barbara," I slurred. Brendan poured me in the front door. I stumbled into the hallway and knocked over the brass umbrella stand. For some reason, Brendan found that very funny.

He laughed. "I can't remember when I've seen you this lit." Brendan steered me toward the stairs.

"I'm perfectly fine."

"Of course you are, sweetheart, but you've had a long day. We both have. Why don't we go take a nap." Brendan practically pushed me up the stairs and into Kitty's room.

"This isn't my room," I protested weakly, as Brendan slipped the linen shift from my shoulders. "I don't think this is a good idea." I moaned as his hands travelled down the front of my body and cupped my still firm breasts. He then gently pushed me onto Kitty's bed. The old bed creaked under our weight. His mouth expertly covered mine and despite the vow I had taken three years earlier not to be seduced by him again, I responded.

Chapter 8

Ellen

I squinted at the mid-day sun. My head pounded and I groaned as I stumbled to the window and pulled the heavy brocade drapes closed. I crawled back into bed and slept for another hour, too shattered by my four martini evening to even wonder where Brendan was.

The phone rang. I reached across the bed with my eyes closed. "Ellen?"

"Yes," I croaked.

"Ellen, where are you? It's after two, and I need to get back to the store."

"Shit, Carol. I'm sorry. I overslept."

"Overslept?"

"Yeah, it's a long story," I said, my voice like gravel.

"I'll call Lisa."

I sat up. "No, give me a half hour."

"Ellie, I can't. That stupid teenager will likely leave, if he hasn't left already and Danny's in Queens with a supplier. Look, she's asleep. She won't even notice I'm gone."

"Okay, Carol, you go. I'll get there as soon as I can." I placed the phone in its cradle and then made my way to the bathroom. I stood in a stream of hot water but felt faint and finished the rest of my shower sprawled on the rough scarred porcelain of the ancient tub. I eventually climbed out of the tub and wrapped my aching body in a threadbare towel. I wiped the small mirror. Eyes, slightly bloodshot, cheeks raw from Brendan's stubble. Lovely.

I walked into my childhood bedroom and threw on a pair of khakis and a white t-shirt and then rubbed a generous dab of my expensive face cream onto my broken skin.

Three aspirin and two cups of coffee later, I was ready to leave for St. Francis. I searched for my car keys. They weren't on the hallway table where I usually keep them. My head throbbed as I searched the house. Reluctantly, I went back upstairs to the scene of the crime and cringed when I saw my green linen dress crumpled in the middle of the room, my sandals and bra beside it. My keys were on the bedside table, a torn piece of paper underneath them.

E,
Great night,
B.

I looked around the room—all trace of Brendan were gone. That bastard. He must've left for D.C. with no intention of coming back. I'd assumed he'd work out of the New York office for the next few days. How could I be so stupid to even be surprised?

Without time to wallow in my regrets, I returned downstairs, grabbed my bag and a pair of sunglasses and walked out of the house. I swooned slightly as I walked down the front steps and had to grab the iron railing for support. With no breeze, the air was hot, muggy and tinged with the stench of rotting seaweed. A wave of nausea hit me, but I fought it as I walked, slowly, to my car.

"Hey, Ellen."

Oh, no. Not another encounter with the beautiful Billy when I looked like I'd been dragged backwards through a hedge. I couldn't very well pretend I didn't hear him. With a smile that almost cracked my sore face, I managed to say hello.

"Ellen, you okay?"

"Yeah, I had a few too many drinks with my husband last night."

"Your husband came up? I thought there was a German carmakers convention here on Rose Hill."

I laughed, and then winced from the pain in my head.

"Ellen, you sure you're okay to drive? I can give you a ride if you like."

I'll bet you could, I thought. Oh man, one sexual experience in three years, and now I'd turned into a sex maniac, in my head anyway. I drove thoughts of a shirtless Billy from my mind and said, "That's very kind of you, but I'll need my car later."

"Okay, whatever you say. See you around, and stay off the sauce," he scolded.

"Don't worry. I think I've learned my lesson," I said as I sank into the hot leather seats of my much mocked car.

Twenty minutes later, I walked, somewhat unsteadily, down the cool tile halls of St. Francis. Molly's voice boomed from my mother's room. Great, that's all I needed.

"Here she is now, Rosie. I told you she'd be along soon."

"Hi Mom. Hi Molly," I said, with a bright fake smile. "Sorry I'm late, but I had to see Brendan off."

My mother's face fell. "He had to go back already?"

"Yes, and he was so disappointed," I lied, "but they needed him back in D.C. His insider trading case is really heating up."

"I'm sure he's indispensable," Molly said drily, her finely honed bullshit detector clearly going off.

"I'm sure he'll call you soon, Mom."

"Tell him not to worry about me," Rose said. "He should concentrate on his work."

"Okay, Rose, time for your bath," a big blond nurse's aide announced as she entered the room. "Ladies, if you'll excuse us."

"Sure," I said, "we'll just go outside for a few minutes."

Molly and I walked out of the room and down to the courtyard. Once there, I collapsed onto one of the wooden benches.

"Tough night last night?"

"A little too much wine at dinner last night, that's all," I said, not a little defensively.

"Well, Sarah's going out clubbing tonight with her friends. Perhaps you'd like to tag along?"

"Very funny, Molly. Look, I had a little too much to drink last night, so sue me."

"I don't care if you drink a gallon of vodka every night, so long as you're here during you assigned times and that woman is not left alone. I thought that's what we all agreed was best for Rose, for her not to be left alone."

"Carol was here until two and I got here at 3:30. She was asleep when Carol left."

"And when I got here she was awake and alone, staring out the window," Molly snapped.

"For heaven's sake, give me a break. I took a leave of absence from work, my children are getting themselves ready to go back to college. I'm here day and night doing the best I can."

"Showing up like something the cat dragged in is the best you can do?"

55

I stood up and fought the nausea from the sudden movement. For a moment I stared at Molly, her thin lips set in a prim, disapproving line. She really was a self righteous bitch, one who would always find fault with me no matter what I did. All my weeks of placating her and playing by her rules had gotten me nowhere. Well, enough was enough. "Molly, I am tired of you and your attitude. We've got a few more weeks together at most and then we never have to see each other again so why don't you keep all your advice and opinions to yourself." I stormed out of the courtyard and walked to the cafeteria for a cup of coffee.

Fifteen minutes later, I returned to my mother's room. She was comfortably dozing. A few moments later, Molly walked into the room.

I said blankly, "Molly, why don't you go home. I'll stay until Paul shows up for the night shift."

Molly sat beside me. "I don't want to keep fighting with you. This is a time when family should stick together."

"I don't want to fight with you either. I know I haven't been the best daughter, but maybe that's because she wasn't the best mother. I know that she's sweet and good, but she didn't give me the one thing I always wanted. A father. But, I suppose that's neither here nor there." I looked at Rose and continued, "I'm just trying to do the right thing by her now, and I can't do that if you point out my every shortcoming."

"You're right. I'm sorry. This is just so hard," her voice broke. "I've spent my life protecting her, and I can't stop now."

"I know, Molly. I know how much you love her."

We sat there for a few moments and looked at my sleeping mother. Then Molly moved closer to me and said in a low voice, "Denis Lenihan was my husband's partner for close to ten years. He retired about five years ago. Last time I saw him was at my Bobby's wake. He and his wife live on Bluebell Lane in Levittown, although they talked about moving to Florida. That's all I know."

I looked at Molly, stunned. My elusive father has lived fifteen miles away from Rose Hill all this time. "Thank you," I managed to say.

Molly nodded.

Chapter 9

Rose

The soft breeze moved the now familiar veil across my face. I bent to pull another weed. Mother Mary Ignatius discovered my green thumb and had assigned me to vegetable garden duty. I was grateful, given my rambunctious friend, Sister Elizabeth, had pulled latrine duty. A car door slammed in the distance. We didn't receive many mid-week visitors. I squinted but without my glasses couldn't see beyond the garden gate. I bent down again and attacked the hard ground with my hoe.

Twenty minutes later my friend Elizabeth walked towards me. "You're wanted in Mother's office." The fact that she spoke at all worried me; Wednesdays were our day of silence.

"What's going on, Lizzie?"

"I don't know. She said to come right away."

I returned my gardening basket to the shed and after I washed my hands in the scullery sink hurried to Mother's office.

"Sister Rose, please come in," Mother said kindly.

"Mama?"

Kitty and Paul sat on the chairs next to Mother's mahogany desk.

Mother Mary Ignatius led me to an empty chair. "Your mother has some very sad news."

I looked at Kitty. She'd refused to even say good-bye to me when I left, and it was Auntie Margaret and Uncle John who drove me the six hours to Our Lady of Angels convent.

"It's Peter. He's had a stroke."

"Is he..."

"No, he's not dead," Kitty said matter-of-factly. "He collapsed last week and was released from the hospital two days ago. Auntie Margaret is staying with him now. He's paralyzed, and can barely speak. The doctors say his mind hasn't been affected, more's the shame for him. There's no hope of recovery."

"I'm sorry, Mama," I said, not feeling the least bit sorry. "But why are you here?"

She looked over at Mother Mary Ignatius, who said, "Your family needs you, Sister."

My stomach clenched. With effort, I choked out, "But, I'm a nun now. I live here."

"You're a postulant, Sister. You know you haven't taken your final vows."

"But I'm a good nun, Mother. I belong here."

"You have done wonderfully these past few months, my child. But, sometimes God has other plans for us. Your place is with your family."

I turned to my mother. "Why do you need me? What do you want me to do about all this?"

Kitty seemed surprised by my truculence. She reached for my hand but I snatched it away. "I have two young children, a business and an invalid husband. My sisters have their own families and their own responsibilities. Rosie, love, I have no one but you."

"No, I won't go." Tears streamed down my cheeks.

"Don't make me beg, Rosie." Mama wiped the tears from my face.

"Your place is with your family, Sister," Mother Mary Ignatius said. "In time, if things settle down with your family, you can return to us."

I looked hard at Kitty. I'd escaped her once. I knew if I left with her now, I'd never return to my beloved convent in the mountains.

"Fine," I said. "Let's go."

With a heavy heart, I climbed the polished marble stairs to the first years dormitory. I fought back tears and I packed my few belongings in the too large empty suitcase Kitty gave me.

"Please tell me you're not leaving," Sister Elizabeth said from the doorway.

"My stepfather's had a stroke."

"Rosie, you can't leave me. I'll never make it here without you."

I looked over at my good friend who had cried every night with homesickness for our first three months, a concept incomprehensible to me. Lizzie, who constantly fought Sister Mary Michael, our dorm supervisor. Poor Lizzie, who's spirit was nearly broken by latrine duty and endless hours spent peeling potatoes.

"I'll send you chocolates," I promised.

"You know those old bats will just eat them themselves. Ah, Rosie, promise me you'll hurry back."

"I'll try," I choked out, knowing that absent a miracle, I'd never be back.

Two weeks later, the house on Rose Hill settled into its new routine. Kitty took over Peter's responsibilities at the hardware store and the boys helped out after school. Kitty, who Peter had forbidden to work at the store early in their marriage after he caught her flirting with the customers, was clearly in her element. Like a woman possessed, she scoured the dusty, neglected store from top to bottom. She straightened the shelves, held a sale to get rid of old, outdated merchandise, and graced every customer who walked in the door with a big County Kerry hello and her undivided attention. Receipts had already increased.

Now I was the prisoner of Rose Hill. Aside from trips to the grocery and the drug stores, I rarely left the house. Day after day I spoon fed the hateful Peter, wiped the spittle from his frozen face, and lifted the dead weight of his body while he relieved himself in a bedpan. "Imagine you are caring for Jesus," Mother Superior had counseled before I left the convent. Giving the old bastard his daily sponge bath, it was hard to imagine Jesus' face in place of the man who'd beaten me senseless more than once.

As weeks turned to months, my revulsion at washing his crepey flesh only increased. Kitty, the trained nurse, never once took a turn. Kitty, who would stick her head into the small room maybe once a day and shout a "How ya love" at him on her way out the door, had blossomed. My mother no longer had that haunted look. Her hair grew in, luscious and thick, and her cheeks became round and rosy. Me, on the other hand, I was as thin as a wraith. I looked like the middle-aged wreck while she looked like the carefree teenager.

"Sorry, Rose," the aide said as she rubbed the rough sponge along my back, "I know this can be uncomfortable. I'm almost done."

"Not at all," I assured her, shaking myself from my thoughts. "I know you haven't an easy job." I knew only too well how washing sick old flesh, day in and day out, could sicken and wither your own soul.

She turned me over and smiled. "All done now. Feel better?"

I returned her smile. "Yes, thank you." Ellen entered the room, her face like thunder, followed by the equally agitated Molly. I feigned sleep. After a while I really did doze, but then I, I heard the name Denis Lenihan. My eyelids fluttered. No, I must have misheard. Molly would never tell Ellen my secret. But my head was foggy and I couldn't help but release myself to the comforting oblivion of sleep.

Chapter 10

Ellen

I circled the block one more time. A young Indian woman wheeling a baby carriage stared at me. Perhaps she thought I was lost. I smiled at her out my car window and made a left on Daisy Lane, a left on Daffodil Way and then another left back onto Bluebell Lane. Number 14 was a tidy cape cod with white aluminum siding and blood red shutters. While the last four times I drove past, its small front yard was empty, this time a tall dark-haired man in his early thirties dragged a dented garbage pail down its short driveway. I pulled in front of the house and rolled down my window.

"Excuse me, do you know Denis Lenihan?"

He looked up, his dark eyes curious. "Yes, I'm Denis Lenihan. Can I help you with something?"

"Oh," I sputtered, "I'm sorry. But, ah, the Denis Lenihan I'm looking for is in his sixties, at least."

"That would be my dad."

"Is he around? I'm Bobby Connelly's niece, you know, his ex-partner?"

His expression warmed. "Sure, I knew Bobby. He was the captain at the Eight-Four when I was a rookie. I'm sorry, but my dad's out in California this week visiting my sister. You wanna leave a message?"

"No, that's okay."

"You sure?"

"Yes, I'm, uh, doing some research and my Aunt Molly thought he might be able to help me."

"He'll be back next week. Give Molly my regards."

Research? How stupid did that sound? I'd never make a good spy, that's for sure. As I drove past the curious Indian woman one more time, tears slid down my cheek. God, I needed to get hold of myself. I'd waited forty-three years to meet my father, surely another week wouldn't make much difference.

I turned left onto Hempstead Turnpike and drove past endless strip malls. How was it possible that my mysterious father lived among such mundane surroundings? As a child I'd pictured him as a Texan ranch hand, an international spy, even a mountain climber; someone who's exotic profession prevented him from visiting me. Visions of him driving his kids around in a station wagon and stopping at the local supermarket for milk was a bit of let down.

I drove the twenty minutes to Centerport and suppressed the urge to head to the airport; part of me wanted to hop on a plane and track my father down in California. I pulled into my mother's driveway, cranky and annoyed.

"Ellen!"

Lisa puffed her way up the slight incline from the boat house to the driveway. Without the energy to be civil, I snapped, "Yes?"

Out of breath, Lisa asked, "Did you get my messages?" For the past week, Lisa had left me almost daily messages, but I deleted them as soon as I heard her voice.

"Yeah, I meant to call you."

"I know you have so much on your plate right now, but really, the neighbors are going to start talking."

"The neighbors? What are you talking about, Lisa?"

"The lawn. I mean look at the state of it. The Historical Society's Annual Tour is next week."

"So?"

"So, how can you expect to be part of the tour with the garden like that?"

"Okay, now you've lost me, Lisa."

Lisa placed her hands on her ample hips. "Rose's house and Barbara Conroy's house, along with the Feinstein's house down the street have been part of the tour for the last four years."

"Oh, for the love of God, nobody will expect us to be part of that now."

"The flyers have the house listed. I saw one last week, as I said on my message. Listen, why don't I send my gardener over. He can get this cleaned up in no time."

Out of pique, I stupidly said, "No, Lisa, I've got it. In fact, I had planned on doing some gardening this afternoon."

"Some gardening, Ellen? That grass looks like it's at least a foot tall."

"It's not that bad. I need the exercise anyway." I moved toward the front door. "Well, I'd better get started."

Lisa looked baffled but I ignored her and walked into the house. I waited until her minivan drove away before I stepped outside again. How could I be such an idiot? I reluctantly made my way to the shed. The small midges that always swarmed the front garden at low tide attacked my bare arms. I eyed the ancient hand mower and wondered how was it possible that my family owned a hardware store, yet this mower was older than me? I pulled the rusted mower from the shed and scraped my elbow against the rough wooden door of the shed. Drops of blood landed on my white t-shirt. I dragged the mower over to the lawn and pushed it with all my might, which given that I hadn't been to the gym in weeks, wasn't much. The grass was so high I couldn't mow more than a foot or so before I had to stop and pull ropes of grass from the mower's dull blades. After an hour, not even a quarter of the small lawn was cut. My white t-shirt was almost transparent with sweat.

"Hey Ellen, how ya doing?" I heard over the hedge.

"Fantastic, thanks to your mother and that goddamned historical society."

"Whoa, what's going on?"

"I'm trying to cut this fucking jungle with a scissors, that's what's going on."

A few moments later, Billy appeared on my lawn, dressed in a tank top and a pair of well worn, and snug, jeans. "Why don't you go inside and get me a beer?"

"Get you a beer? I'm a little busy here."

"Get me a beer, Ellen. I like to drink a beer while I mow."

"You don't need to..."

He eyed my t-shirt and smirked. "Just go."

My arms throbbed and my face burned from exertion and the beginnings of a sunburn. Like a petulant teenager, I threw down the handle of the mower and stomped inside. The hallway's cool air felt good against my sweat-soaked skin. I stripped off my wet t-shirt in the kitchen and grabbed a wrinkled, but clean, blue t-shirt from the dryer. I splashed some water on my face before I slipped on the shirt. Feeling marginally better, I grabbed two cold beers from the fridge and walked back outside. In the meantime, Billy had gotten his mother's gas mower and had already started on the lawn. I walked over and handed him the beer. He smiled and took it from me without breaking his stride. I got out of his way and returned to the steps and drank my beer. Less than twenty minutes later, the lawn was done. Billy switched off the mower, walked over to me, his jeans now slung low on his hips and said, "That, Miss Murphy, is how you mow a lawn. Now get me another beer and I'll help you weed."

"Really, Billy, you don't..."

"Beer. Now."

I returned to the kitchen and brought out two more beers. Billy finished his in two long gulps. In another hour, the two of us cleared the flower beds of their weeds, and if the garden didn't look the same as it did under Rose's watch, it at least looked respectable.

"Not bad," he said. "Tomorrow I'll help you with the back."

"You really don't..."

"Tomorrow I'll mow the back," he said firmly with a smile.

I laughed. "Okay, okay, I won't bother arguing with you, but, I need to repay you. Let me buy you dinner."

"I have a better idea. I was supposed to meet a buddy of mine an hour ago. Why don't you buy us a pitcher of beer at Gunther's."

"A pitcher? I don't think I've bought a pitcher of beer since law school."

"Sorry, sweetheart, but they don't sell carafes of wine at Gunther's Tap House."

I smiled. "Okay, okay. A pitcher it is. If you play your cards right, I may even throw in some peanuts."

"That's my girl. Let's go."

"All right, let me get my keys."

He eyed my silver sedan. "I don't think they'll serve us if we show up in that thing. I've got my bike."

"I can follow you."

"Come on, Ellen, where's your sense of adventure? I have an extra helmut. You can ride with me."

"Well, I, uh, I don't know."

"What's the matter, El? You afraid?"

"I'm not afraid. Well, not too afraid." I looked at the motorcycle for a moment. It appeared sturdy enough. "What the hell, let me get my bag and lock up." Running into the house, I quickly brushed my hair, slathered on some face cream to sooth the sunburn

64

and grabbed my bag. Before I had a chance to reconsider, I found myself on the back of Billy's motorcycle, my legs snug against his, roaring down Rose Hill.

The bike was steady and Billy was a good rider, although I suspected he was riding slower than usual for my benefit. I relaxed enough to enjoy the quick ride to Northport village. By the time we pulled in front of Gunther's deliberately dingy entrance, I was almost disappointed we'd arrived so quickly.

"So you survived your first ride?" Billy asked as he pulled off his helmut and ran his hand through his shaggy hair.

"How do you know this is my first ride on a motorcycle?" I struggled to undo the strap of the helmut. "Perhaps I have a wild and sordid past that you know nothing about."

Billy smiled. "You forget, Miss Homecoming Queen of 1985, I was there for your past."

"All right, you got me. Let's go get that beer." I tried to fix my hopelessly messy hair.

"Here, let me." Billy patted the left side of my head. "There, much better. Oh, I meant to tell you, I like the new lid."

"You do?"

"Yes, it suits you. Now come on. If the guys find me out here discussing hairstyles, I'll never hear the end of it." He opened the flimsy screen door. "After you."

It took a few moments for my eyes to adjust to the dark interior of the bar. Not much had changed since Laurie Nolan and I, armed with the pathetic fake IDs we'd bought in Times Square, braved the local biker bar. I smiled when I saw the corner table Laurie and I had once commandeered and preened for the grizzled bikers, our big hair somehow defying gravity.

"Bud okay?" Billy asked as we approached the crowded bar.

"Do they have Amstel?"

"Oh, I should have known. Fancy imported car, fancy imported beer." Catching the bartender's eye, he said, "Hey Jimmy, you got Amstel on tap?"

"I got Heineken."

"That okay?" Billy asked. I nodded, slightly intimidated by the amount of testosterone in the crowded bar.

"One pitcher of Heineken, Jimmy. Hey Jimmy, you seen Vince around?"

"Yeah, he left about twenty minutes ago."

"Was that your friend? I'm sorry that you missed him."

Billy smiled. "Don't worry about it. You're a much better looking drinking companion. Let's see if we can snag a table in the back."

Billy carried the pitcher while I trailed him carrying two frosted mugs. I pretended not to notice the appreciative glances he garnered from the two pseudo biker chicks who leaned seductively against the battered pool table. We pushed against a crowd of preppy college kids home for the summer. Billy expertly maneuvered his way to the back where he found a small scarred table in the corner.

"Here we go." He held out a small wooden chair for me.

"It's pretty packed tonight."

"Yeah, I usually avoid Friday nights here." He poured us both a glass. "I guess dive bars aren't exactly your scene anymore, huh?"

"Not really, although it's nice for a change." I bravely ate a handful of trail mix from a small plastic bowl.

"What do you and your husband usually do together?" Billy grabbed a large handful of the trail mix.

"Not much." I didn't mean for that to slip out.

"Oh."

What the hell, I might as well come clean. It wasn't as if Billy knew anyone from my "real life" in D.C. I took a deep breath and then said, "We go to brunch occasionally and of course I make an appearance at certain mandatory spouse functions at his law firm. Brendan is a big fan of musical theatre, which I don't really love, so he usually takes one of his girlfriends."

"Girlfriends?"

"Yeah," I said evenly.

"And you're okay with that?"

I shrugged. "I wasn't at first, of course. But, by the time I finally acknowledged Brendan's cheating, it had been going on for years and he wasn't about to change. I had three young children, who when he was around, adored their father. I had a choice to make. Either maintain my principles and leave him, destroying my children's childhood in the process, or stick it out. I know what it's like to grow up without a father. Brendan might not have been the best father in the world, but he was their father, and I didn't want to deprive them of that."

66

"I'm divorced and I'm still a father to my son."

"Yes, but that's because you're probably committed to being a father. As it was, even living in the same house, the children barely saw him. It would have been worse if we'd divorced."

"So, do you two..."

"No," I said. "Our, ah, physical relationship ended years ago." Well, excluding last week, but I didn't feel like being that honest with Billy.

"Sorry, Ellen, I really don't mean to pry, it's just that I find it unbelievable that anyone would cheat on you. He must be either crazy or blind."

"I put up with it so I guess I'm the crazy one."

"No, Ellen, no." His large callused hand covered mine. "You're just a good mother."

I shook my head. "You make me sound like a saint. No, since we're being completely honest, I have to admit that I get something out of the relationship too, such that it is. We travel in very exclusive circles, belong to a country club, live in a multi-million dollar home. I suppose part of me doesn't want to give that up, and admit that my picture perfect life is less than perfect."

"I think you're being too hard on yourself."

"No, just honest. For once." I sipped from my mug. "Hey, did Gunther put truth serum in this beer or what?"

He laughed. "God, let's hope not, or I would've gotten into trouble a long time ago."

I picked up the empty pitcher. "Are you up for another?"

"Sure, why not."

The bar had gotten even more crowded, but I was able to fight my way to the bar and grab bartender Jimmy's attention. As I made my way past the pool table, one of the young preppy dudes bumped against me and beer splashed on my shirt. One of the pseudo biker chicks who looked like she was about to pounce on Billy scowled at me when I pushed past her to take my seat.

"Here we go." I poured the beer into the mugs.

Billy laughed. "Hey, thanks for the foam. You obviously haven't poured a pitcher in a while." He took the pitcher from my hand. "Here, let me."

"Sorry. I'm sure one of my sons can give me a lesson when I get home."

"No worries." He expertly tipped the glass so that it filled with beer and not bubbles. "I promise this will be the last personal question of the night, but if you and your husband aren't, how should I put it, intimate, then what do you do for, uh..."

"Companionship?"

"Yes. You're a beautiful woman."

I laughed. "I'm covered in beer and sweat, so I'm not feeling particularly beautiful at the moment."

"Don't look for more compliments, El, you know what I mean."

"There was someone a few years ago. One of the divorced dads at my daughter's school. We were very discreet, but I don't know, it wasn't for me. I couldn't compartmentalize my feelings in that way. He wanted to take it further, wanted me to see him more openly, and I used that as an excuse to break up with him. I don't think Brendan wouldn't have cared if I saw someone, and even if he did, he certainly wasn't in any position to complain." I paused for a moment and looked down at my beer. "It was me. I didn't want to be the type of woman who had affairs. I didn't want my children to see me as that type of person," I looked up then into Billy's compassionate gaze. "Stupid, huh?"

"No," Billy said, "it doesn't sound stupid to me. It sounds very lonely, though."

"It is, at times. But, I have my children and my work." We sat together silently then, and sipped the cold sudsy beer.

Billy smiled. "Hey, the pool table's open. You wanna play?"

"Sure, although I'm not very good."

"Come on." He took my hand and led me to the pool table. We played two college kids, and thanks to Billy's moves, we beat them and the next two contenders as well. I smiled as Billy talked sports with the first set of college kids, construction tips with the second, middle-aged group. Billy was unpretentious and friendly and I felt completely at ease with him in this grungy bar, despite my earlier confessions.

Two pitchers later, I was ready to call it a night. I didn't want a repeat of my previous boozy evening. Billy gently placed his hand on my lower back and guided me through the still crowded bar. Once outside, I headed to the bike.

"Ellen, I'm sorry but I don't think I'm in any shape to take you home on that. I got a DWI last year so I don't want to risk it."

68

"That's okay, I'll just take a cab."

"Where do you think you are, Manhattan? Let's walk back to my place and I'll call you a cab from there. I only live a few blocks away."

We walked in companionable silence along Northport's main thoroughfare, past the overpriced boutiques, ice cream parlors and nautically inspired gift shops. Two blocks from the harbor, we turned right and walked another three blocks until we reached a pale yellow clapboard Victorian. Billy took my hand and we walked up the steep narrow brick steps to the front door. Inside was one big construction site, with only the kitchen marginally habitable.

"I know, I know, but in my defense counselor, I'm so busy working on other people's houses I never have time to finish my own. I do have a refrigerator that works, though. What would you like to drink? Wine? Beer?"

"Coffee, if you have it."

"Sure. Wait on the deck, and I'll be right out." Billy opened French doors that led to a large wooden deck. Outside, the air was warm and I sank into a lounge chair. I was buzzed but unlike my night with Brendan, still in control.

"Here we go." Billy placed a large tray on the side table next to the lounge chair and then sat next to me.

As he handed me the coffee, I asked, "So how long have you lived here?"

"About three years. I moved here after my divorce, but I only started ripping it apart six months ago. It'll be nice when it's finished. If it ever gets finished, that is."

"It must be exciting to renovate your own house. I imagine it must be liberating, not to ask your wife what kind of tile she wants, if you should use granite or marble."

"Yeah, but it's kind of weird too. I guess that's why I lived with wood paneling for two years before I did something about it. I never thought at this stage of my life I'd be living alone. It's freeing, but sad at the same time. You know what I mean?"

"Yeah. I think I do."

We sipped our coffee, silent except for the cacophony of cicadas. My hand brushed against his as I placed my empty mug on the table. He looked at me, his eyes almost glowed in the moonlight. My breath quickened as he reached over and touched my shoulder.

He pulled me closer and kissed me, tenderly at first and then more forcefully, urgently.

"I've been wanting to do that for weeks, Miss Murphy," he said softly.

"I know. Me too." I leaned forward to kiss him again. His hand softly brushed against my right breast.

A neighbor's back door slammed. "Maybe we should move this inside."

"I think you should call me a cab now. If you don't call it soon, I might not leave and I really think I should go."

"I wish you wouldn't," he murmured in my ear.

"I have to be at St. Francis early tomorrow. But that's not really the reason. I just, I just don't want to make a mistake here."

"Does this feel like a mistake?" Billy kissed me again.

For some reason, panic overwhelmed me. I pushed him away. "Please Billy, I think I should go."

He looked at me for a moment, his eyes surprised and not a little hurt. "Of course." He stood up. "Let me find the number." He walked into the house.

Not knowing whether to be disappointed or relieved at his acquiescence, I followed him into the house.

Chapter 11

Rose

    The morning sun blinded me, even through the thin shades the nurses had not yet opened. It was too early for breakfast. And too early for my morphine shot as well. The jagged edge of pain the morphine kept partially at bay was sharper now. I grimaced, but did not call out. For the past few days I'd tried to pretend that the pain was not so bad so that they wouldn't place me on the continuous drip Sister Elizabeth told me would be the next step in my pain management. Medication brought relief, but at a terrible price. It made me disoriented, sleepy. I didn't have much time left, but what little I did have, I wanted to be awake for. Cogent. So that I could talk with my daughter.

    Although our conversations these past few weeks had carefully skimmed the surface, I could sit in this room and listen to Ellen read the phone book. That would be enough for me. I doubted it would be enough for her.

    I looked with distaste at the large vase full of carnations next to my bed. Their stench overpowered the room. I'll tell Ellen to throw them out. Carnations. In my mind's eye I saw my mother pin an obnoxious corsage onto my graduation dress.

    "See, Rosie. I had them dyed to match your dress."

    "Oh, I didn't know carnations came in blue." I kept the disappointment from my voice. Peter stood next to her and I didn't want to give him an excuse to make a scene.

    "Red, blue, yellow," Kitty said brightly. "Every color."

    I tried to ignore the other graduates who wandered the halls holding their bouquets of roses.

    "Darling," my mother said to Peter. "Could you help me with this?" Out of a plastic bag my mother pulled out an even bigger corsage that consisted of at least a half dozen yellow roses. "Doesn't this match my dress perfectly?" Kitty asked me.

    "Yes," I said without inflection. "It's perfect."

The squeak of the heavy door to my room brought me back. "Morning, Rosie."

"Good morning, Sister."

"How many times do I have to tell you, knock it off with this Sister business."

I laughed. "Okay. Good morning, Lizzie."

"Much better." Lizzie sat down next to my bed.

"What are you doing here so early?" I asked.

"Mae Broderick down the hall. She passed about an hour ago." Lizzie's face was pale, tired.

"How long was she here?" I asked.

"Three months."

"That was longer than they thought she'd last, wasn't it?"

"Yes."

"I might make it to three months," I said hopefully.

"Maybe." She paused for a moment. "Rose, why are you so anxious for the extra time? Many of the patients here are scared of what comes next. They don't have faith, or they frantically grab for it in the end. But you, Rosie, your faith is strong. Stronger than my own. It always has been. So why do you want the extra time when you know it will only involve more pain?"

"I want more time with Ellen," I choked out, my throat suddenly dry. "I need to make things right with her."

"I know you feel guilty about Ellen, but honestly, you have to let that go. You did a good job with her. She's well educated....."

"She's well educated," I interrupted, "thanks to you. I don't know what I would've done if you hadn't arranged that scholarship."

"Rosie, you don't need to thank me." Lizzie patted my hand. "I made few calls. What's the point of having an uncle who's a Jesuit if you can't pull a few strings? And besides, she did Boston College proud. Ellen got into law school all by herself, now she has that big government job. That was all her."

"Yes, but if you hadn't helped. Hadn't gotten her out of that house when you did..."

"Maybe she wouldn't be such a bossy miss if she had married the boy down the street. But, ah, who's to know. You make the best decision you can at the time and leave the rest up to God, right? And everything worked out. She's accomplished, successful, happy."

72

"She's not happy. I don't think she's ever been happy, not really."

"Ellen's an adult now with grown children of her own. Her happiness is her own responsibility, Rose, not yours."

"I suppose you're right." I couldn't say to my childless friend, you're not a mother, you could never understand.

Lizzie leaned towards me. "Is there something else, Rose? Some other reason you're uneasy?"

I spent two years wishing for a helpless old man's death, I wanted to say. I watched him choke to death and did nothing to stop it. No priest's absolution could adequately pardon me of that crime. How could I say that to my friend, my friend who'd put my faith and steadfastness on a pedestal all these years? Instead, I shook my head. "It's hard, Lizzie. Even with my faith. It's difficult to let go."

"Of course it is, Rose." She patted my bony hand. "Forgive me if I upset you."

Pain now split my head in two. "There's nothing to forgive," I whispered.

"You need your medicine. Let me get the nurse." Lizzie hurried out of the room. Relief washed through me. My medication would be here soon; no nurse could say no to the persistent Sister Elizabeth.

Lizzie had been a good friend to me over the years, but she never understood my relationship with my daughter. I made her promise not to tell Ellen about our role in the scholarship. "But, Rosie," Lizzie said at the time, "isn't this the solution to all your problems with Ellen? This will bring you closer."

"You can't tell her we were involved. There's no way she'll go to Boston College if she thinks I'm behind it."

"I don't understand."

"That's right, Lizzie, you don't. And consider yourself lucky you don't."

Lizzie abided by my edict and to this day Ellen still had no idea Lizzie and I were the catalyst behind her great academic career. And her escape from Rose Hill.

When the envelope from Boston College arrived, I placed it back in the mailbox for Ellen or my mother to find. Ellen, trailed by Johnny Griffin from down the street, found the letter. She carelessly threw it on the kitchen counter before she retreated to her room with

Johnny where they did God knew what. Johnny was tall, dark and dumb, which was Ellen's taste at the time. He was a freshman at Hofstra University, only twenty minutes from Centerport, and he had been lobbying heavily for Ellen to stay home for college. Kitty was friends with his mother and they were both delighted that the kids were dating. Kitty did everything in her power to push the romance along. Ellen, married and local and still under her thumb, would've been a dream come true for my mother.

Well, not if I could help it. Ellen had been lackadaisical when it came to her college applications. She'd left it up to me to type most of them. It was easy enough to slip Boston College among her other applications.

Later, after dinner, my mother sifted through the mail.

"Ellie," she called, "you have mail."

I busied myself with folding laundry at the kitchen table when Ellen floated into the kitchen. She picked through the mail and spent an inordinate amount of time flipping through a catalog. She finally opened the Boston College letter.

"Mom, did I apply to Boston College?"

"Hmm, I think you might have. Although I don't know why. There's no way I'd let you go there."

"Why not?" she said. "Laurie Nolan's cousin went there and had a blast."

"Exactly," I sniped. "That's why you're not going. Plus, it's way too expensive."

Ellen threw the letter in front of me. "They've offered me a scholarship so it shouldn't be too expensive."

I looked at Kitty. "Mama," I said to her, "can you help me out here? I thought we decided that Ellen was going to Hofstra."

Ellen's fair cheeks flamed with temper. "You decided? You two decided where I'm going to college?"

Kitty for once looked confused. "But, Ellie, I thought you wanted to go to Hofstra and stay home with Johnny?"

Ellen flipped her long blond hair out of her eyes. "Laurie's cousin said the boys at BC are hot."

I stood up and threw the towel I had been folding on the table. "If you think I'm going to allow you to move hundreds of miles away to do God knows what with boys in your dorm room, you've got another thing coming, missy. Right, Mama?"

Kitty looked uncertainly at Ellen. She wasn't used to siding with me against Ellen. My mother liked to be the good guy when it came to my daughter. "Well, I don't know, Rosie. If it's a good school and free and all, maybe we should think about it."

"Over my dead body!" I stormed out of the kitchen and prayed I hadn't overplayed my hand. It turned out I hadn't. By the next week Ellen had sent back her acceptance letter and a four short months later she was packed off to college, away from Johnny Griffin and out of that house.

The sharp pain emanating from my left eye socket brought me back to my room. I couldn't prevent the tears that soon streamed down my poor withered face. I cried for my pain. I cried for the few days left to me. I cried for my guilt. I cried for the daughter who would never know how much I loved her.

"Mom, you okay? Should I get the nurse?" For once, Ellen had turned up on time.

I controlled my sobs and attempted a smile. "Sister Elizabeth has gone to get her. They should be back soon."

"What can I do? Mom, just tell me what you want me to do."

"Sing to me, Ellen. Sing to me until they get here."

Ellen picked up the battered missalette Lizzie had swiped from the chapel and flipped through it to find something she recognized. Soon, her sweet soprano sang a song I recognized from her Holy Communion. I remembered when she sang it for me and Mama in the kitchen, every night for weeks.

"Let there be peace on Earth, and let it begin with me..."

Ellen continued to sing her childish song even after the nurse entered and delivered a shot of relief. Even after my eyes closed.

Later I woke, alone. I fumbled for my glasses. Outside my window, Ellen and Sister Elizabeth sat together in the courtyard, deep in conversation. Maybe Lizzie could give Ellen some comfort. God knows, I couldn't.

Chapter 12

Ellen

Sister Elizabeth held out a pack of cigarettes. "Do you want one?"

"You smoke?"

She laughed. "Yeah, I'm the smoking nun. Let me know if you see Nurse Collins, she's a devil for enforcing the rules."

It was nice to know I wasn't the only black sheep at St. Francis. "I will. Did you and my mother sneak ciggies in the convent?"

"Even I'm not that brave. Your mother was a wizard at smuggling in chocolates and chewing gum. I still don't know how she did it. Mother Superior was very strict, especially with the first year postulants. No, I picked up this particular bad habit when I worked as a social worker in San Francisco. But hey, it was the 60s, I could've done a lot worse."

"Bad habits in a convent?"

"Believe me, there were plenty of bad habits to go around. Put twenty women together and you're sure to see plenty. Gossip, petty fights, spitefulness. My smoking was a minor offense. At least now I'm not wearing a habit, so I just look like another nicotine addict. You should've seen the looks I got when I was wearing the penguin suit. Sure I can't tempt you?"

"I'm sure. My neighbor convinced me to ride on a motorcycle and drink a pitcher of beer last night, so I think that's enough decadence for this week." I didn't feel the need to disclose the middle-aged make-out session to the good sister.

"Sounds like fun." Sister Elizabeth blew a ring of smoke.

I laughed. "Now you're just showing off."

"I know. I'm an awful show off. Always have been. I'm the youngest of eight, so I had to do something to stand out."

"Becoming a nun wasn't enough?"

She smiled. "Oh no. They barely noticed I was gone. Well, that's not really true. My mother didn't think I'd last a week so she didn't bother to throw me a going away party. She barely said goodbye. No one thought I'd make it, not even Mother Superior. It wasn't always easy, especially after I took my final vows. I was the youngest nun in the convent by at least twenty years and the older nuns were awful to me."

I shifted my weight to get comfortable on the hard bench. "Did you ever think of dropping out?"

"Oh, all the time, especially that first year at Our Lady of Angels." She dragged on the cigarette. "I swear I wouldn't have made it through the first three months if it wasn't for Rosie. I cried for my mother every night. And I was always getting into trouble. Did your mother tell you how I had latrine duty for a solid year?"

"Latrine duty? Sounds like the army."

"Sometimes it felt like the army too. Except that in the army you at least get a night's leave. Convent life back then was 24-7. But, you must know that. I'm sure your mother told you."

"No. She never talked about it. But then again, she's good at keeping secrets."

Sister Elizabeth gave me a hard, appraising look. "Well, if you have any questions for her, now is the time to ask them."

"Yeah, right. If I dare discuss anything other than the weather with her, Molly will have my head. My marching orders from Molly are to be bright and cheerful and not upset my mother."

"This isn't about Molly. It's about you and your mother. Sure, it won't be easy for you to ask questions and it may not be easy for Rose to answer them, but you'll regret it if you don't ask. Many times I counsel families not to bring up distressing topics when a patient is this close to the end. In this case I believe it would be good for both you and your mother to have an honest conversation about what you feel she's kept from you. You may not like what she has to say, but at least you'll know."

"So we can have closure?"

"Closure. I hate that word." Sister Elizabeth stubbed out her cigarette. "You can't wrap up a forty year relationship in a neat little package with a few words. But, you can be honest with each other, and that's something more than what you have now, isn't it?"

I nodded. Sister Elizabeth lit another cigarette.

"I almost don't know where to begin," I said, my voice husky with emotion. "I don't know her at all. You say my mother broke the rules by sneaking in chocolate? I can't imagine anyone less likely to break a rule. Or to do anything really. She's spent her life in that house on Rose Hill. Gardening. Cooking dinner for my grandmother. Going to mass. What kind of life was that?"

"Is that really who you think your mother is?" Sister Elizabeth asked. "You make her sound like a housekeeper."

"That's what she was, wasn't she? She wasn't a wife. She wasn't much of a mother. What did she ever do other than serve as my grandmother's skivvy."

"I feel sorry for you, Ellen. I really do, and I'm not saying this to hurt your feelings. Rose is one of the strongest, most selfless people I know. She's given up everything to care for her family. Her freedom. Her vocation. Her very life."

"Come on," I scoffed. "You're making her sound like Mother Teresa. This is what I know: she flunked out of the convent because she couldn't hack it. She obviously went out one night, got pregnant and couldn't convince the guy to stick around. Then she hid behind my grandmother for the rest of her life."

"You two do have a lot to discuss. But, I'll tell you what I know about Rose. I know that I wouldn't be a nun today if it wasn't for her. I wouldn't have made it through that first year, and I wouldn't have made it through all these years, when so many of my fellow sisters left, some abandoning the Faith altogether. I couldn't have stuck it out without Rose's constant encouragement, even though for years my only contact with her was through her letters and small gifts of chocolate." She looked at me expectantly, but when I said nothing she continued. "What do you think she's been doing since you left home? She nursed your grandmother once the dementia set it. She was active in her church and in the community. She volunteered here twice a week and started the homeless initiative at St. Ann's. Rose cooked and cleaned for the homeless men who slept in the church basement once a week, did you know that? She may have left the convent, and I will leave it to her to explain the circumstances to you, but she continued her life of service. Service to her family, her community, her God. Rosie's had a beautiful, meaningful life," Sister Elizabeth's voice broke. "I'm sorry that you can't see that."

Sister Elizabeth picked up the cigarette butts at her feet and left me to the solitude of the courtyard, her words reverberating in my skull.

My mother didn't wake up for the rest of the day. I sat in her room for hours and contemplated Sister Elizabeth's words. Lisa relieved me at three and I drove to the house on Rose Hill.

The roar of the mower greeted me. I walked around to the back of the house and found Billy in all his sweaty, shirtless glory. His back muscles were taut as he pushed the lawnmower through the overgrown grass. Billy turned, saw me and gave me a curt nod. That was a bit frosty. Maybe he's hot, it was close to ninety degrees after all. I went into the house and poured us both a glass of lemonade.

"Billy."

He continued mowing and didn't acknowledge me.

"Billy," I said louder.

He turned off the mower and walked over to me.

"It's boiling out here. You must be thirsty."

He took the glass I offered him. "Thanks."

"You didn't have to mow on such a hot day. It could've waited."

"I said I'd take care of it."

"Let me get changed and I'll help you."

"It's all right. I've got it covered," he snapped.

"But Billy, I can't let you do all of this by yourself. I'll only be a minute."

"You'll slow me down. Besides, I'm almost finished." He turned away from me and walked back to the mower.

"Well, at least let me cook you dinner or perhaps we could go out."

He didn't look at me. "I gotta pick up my kid at five."

"Well, how about tomorrow?"

Billy turned back towards me. "Look, Ellen, you don't owe me anything. You don't have to buy me dinner or beer or play pool with me. I'm just doing a neighbor a favor, that's all."

"Is that all I am? A neighbor?"

Billy's brown eyes were a mixture of hurt and anger. "You made it clear last night that's all you want to be."

I walked onto the brown, burnt grass towards him. "Billy, I'm sorry but..."

"No reason to be sorry," he interrupted. "Your mother's dying. You got some type of complicated relationship with your husband. You're going through a hard time. I get it. I don't want to make your life more difficult."

"You haven't made my life more difficult. The truth is, meeting up with you again has been the only good thing that has happened since I came home."

"Maybe I don't want to make my life more difficult. Ellen, I just got my life back on an even keel. My business is doing well, my kid's doing well. I'm not up for this push-pull thing you've got going on." He stepped closer to me and his voice then softened. "You're a beautiful woman, Ellen, but you're married and it seems to me that you plan on staying that way. You already told me you're not into flings, and to tell you the truth, neither am I. Why don't you make this easy on both of us and let me finish up back here and then go. Okay?"

Tears stung my eyes but I fought them back and nodded. I picked the two glasses up from the table and, without looking back at him, walked into the house.

Chapter 13

Ellen

Two days later, I knocked on Denis Lenihan's front door. Denis Junior opened it. "Hey, you're the research lady, right?"

"Yes, I'm Ellen Mills. Is your father in by any chance?"

"Yeah, he got back on Monday. Come in, come in. Take a seat and I'll get him."

"That would be great. Thanks." I walked into the living room and sat on an overstuffed floral couch. Family photos lined almost every available bit of wall space. Denis' wedding photo was closest to me, and based on Denis' long sideburns and his wife's long black hair, it looked like they were married in the mid to late seventies. Was Denis single and available when I was born? A bead of sweat tricked down my t-shirt. What was I doing here? Did I really want to know the answer? Maybe my mother was right to keep me in the dark. Unable to stop myself, I stood up and inspected the family pictures more closely: two dark haired boys in matching baseball uniforms, a blond girl with glasses in a class photo.

Denis Junior walked into the room, a large duffle bag with a NYPD insignia slung over his shoulders. "He'll be down in a few minutes. Listen, I'm late to work, but make yourself at home. Turn on the TV if you like."

My face burned with embarrassment. I couldn't believe he found me snooping. If I had any sense, I would've followed Denis Junior out the door and returned to my home on Rose Hill. I stayed, of course, with my back stiff against the hard cushions of the couch and my hands clenched in tight fists.

Ten minutes later, Denis Lenihan Senior entered the room. He was shorter that I'd expected, shoulders slightly bent, skin ruddy and coarse. He looked closer to seventy than sixty although his light blue eyes were sharp and clear.

He held out his hand. "Hello, Denis Lenihan. You're Molly Connelly's niece?"

I reached out and shook his hand. "Cousin, actually," I said, sounding calmer than I was. "She and my mother are first cousins. I believe you knew my mother, Rose Murphy?"

"No, I don't think so. Can I offer you a drink? I don't keep liquor in the house no more, but maybe some tea, coffee? I think my son has some orange soda in the fridge."

"Soda's fine."

He looked around the room. "Let's talk in the kitchen if you don't mind. I never sit in here. It was more my wife's room."

"Sure." I followed him into a small canary yellow kitchen. The room was hot, with only a window fan to provide relief. I sat at a round wooden table wedged into a corner while Denis found the glasses and the soda. After he poured us both a glass, he sat across from me.

"My son says you're doing some research," he said, his gravelly voice uncertain. "I'm not sure what I can help you with since I retired from the job almost ten years ago. You might have better luck talking with Denis. He's on the job and works narcotics. He's a boss too, made lieutenant last year," Denis said, with some pride. He sipped the soda and then ran his hand through his sparse gray hair. "Me, well, I was never one for tests. I was a patrolman 'til the day I retired. I have some stories I could tell you all right, but I'm not sure what you're interested in."

I reached into my purse. "I'm not doing research. I only told your son that. The real reason I'm here is this." I placed the old creased photo on the table in front of Denis. "That's my mother Rose on the left. I never knew my father. My mother refused to tell me anything about him. She's in hospice now, cancer, and I came across this old photo recently. I asked Molly about it and she gave me your name."

Denis' face went white. "I don't understand. You think I'm your father?"

"Yes."

He stared at the photo. After a moment he looked up and met my steady gaze. "This is the first I'm hearing about this. Bobby Connelly was my partner for years. Why didn't he say nothing?"

"I don't know. I think Molly and my mother swore him to secrecy. I know this must be a shock for you. It was for me as well. But, you don't have to take my word for it." I pulled a folder out of my bag. "Here's some information I found on paternity testing along with a photocopy of the St. Patrick's Day photo. Your doctor can take a cheek swab or a hair sample." Denis' bushy eyebrows knit together in concentration, or a scowl, it was hard to tell.

"Of course, I'd be happy to cover all of the cost," I said.

Denis rose from his chair and without a word left the room. I sat in that hot kitchen for several minutes and sipped the flat soda with my stomach in knots. When he returned, he handed me a framed photo of a young blond bride, her blue eyes wide apart, cheekbones high. She appeared to be taller than me and her chin was more square than mine, but it was clear that we were related.

"You look a lot like my daughter, Anne Marie. I don't need a test. I believe you."

I managed a weak smile. "I'm so relieved."

His eyes narrowed. "So now what? My son told me you drive a fancy car and you look fairly prosperous, so you obviously don't need money, and even if you did you'd be out of luck. Other than my pension and this house, I don't have much."

"Mr. Lenihan, Denis, no. I don't want your money."

"Well, what then? You're in your forties, right? You certainly don't need a daddy at this point in your life."

This wasn't going as I'd planned at all. But, Denis was a cop, I rationalized to myself. Of course he's a little suspicious. In an attempt to appease him, I said in as calm a voice as I could manage, "I want to get to know you, Denis. That's all. I want you to get to know me, know my kids."

He fiddled with the soda cap and refused to look at me. "You seem like a nice lady and I'm sure your kids are great, but I don't think I can give you what you want."

"I don't want much, Denis," I said, trying not to sound too frantic. "I won't take up much of your time."

He rubbed his eyes and then said in a low, toneless voice, "I started drinking before I joined the force. Before I graduated high school. My old man owned three bars in Brooklyn and I started pulling pints as a teenager. I never missed a day's work. Never raised a hand to my wife or my kids. But, that don't seem to matter to my kids. Not Denis, of course. He's on the job. He knows what it's like. But the other two, they barely speak to me. They blame me. For not showing up at baseball games, for talking too loud at Anne Marie's wedding, for how I acted at my wife Annette's funeral and I don't know what else."

"I'm sorry."

Denis barely seemed to hear me as he continued. "After Annette died, my daughter said that she wouldn't let me see my grandkids unless I quit drinking. I been in AA since last March. My son Denis swore to her that I been sober for four months so she agreed to let me visit. We had a good time. No fights, no arguments." He looked up at me. "She kissed me at the airport. Told me she loved me. Told me she was proud of me."

"And you don't want to tell her about a long lost daughter," I said.

"I can't. Denis would understand, but the other two wouldn't. And Denis, he's a big mouth and he'd eventually slip. I can't risk telling him"

"I was born years before you were married. Long before you had a family. Surely your daughter wouldn't see your relationship with my mother as any type of betrayal of your wife."

Denis sighed and his shoulders sagged even further. "Look, I can't even remember meeting your mother. I know that must be hard to hear, but it's true." He picked up the faded photograph, turned it over and read the back. "St. Patrick's Day. I'm sure I had a load on. This is all my daughter would need to see, another example of me gettin' drunk and screwin' up. She'd wonder if there were any other surprises out there. Hell, it makes me wonder too."

I grabbed his hand. "Then we won't tell your children. We can have a relationship without involving them."

He pulled his hand away. "Look girlie, I'm sorry. I just quit drinking after nearly fifty years and I'm barely hanging on here. I'm not capable of being your father."

Tears filled my eyes. I found a business card in my wallet and laid it on the table. "Denis, take my card. In case you change your mind."

My father stared at it. "I won't."

Chapter 14

Ellen

"Hello! Anyone home?" Lisa called out. The front screen door closed with a bang.

I shouted from my bedroom, "I'll be down in a minute."

"You'd better hurry. The tour started twenty minutes ago."

Honestly, that woman will be the death of me. I swiped lipstick across my dry lips and smoothed the front of my tailored linen shirt, already wrinkled from the heat. I looked in the mirror. My eyes were two sunken holes and the bright lipstick only highlighted my dull pallor.

I found Lisa in the kitchen, her tight yellow blouse damp with sweat, huffing and puffing while she complete the arduous task of arranging Ritz crackers and cheap orange cheese on a very fragile looking china platter. Lisa looked up. Heavy makeup formed a line at her chin. "There you are. You do know the tour started at one, don't you?"

"Yes, but Danny was late and I didn't leave St. Francis until 12:30." Did I really have to explain myself to this lunatic?

"Then why didn't you leave earlier? I'm sure Rose would've understood that you had to prepare for the tour."

My limited patience at an end, I snarked, "Oh yes, Lisa, that's right. The tour is my mother's number one priority."

"Rose is very proud of the house being included on the tour, Ellen."

It was Lisa who was proud of the house being on the tour; I couldn't imagine that my shy mother had ever relished allowing her snooty North Shore neighbors to poke through her dark rooms. But, fighting with Lisa was like fighting the weeds that had once again overtaken the garden: pointless. "So what do you need me to do?" I asked in a resigned, but more conciliatory tone.

"There is no ice. How you could survive in a house with no ice I'll never know, but there should be plenty in the boathouse. And bring up some glasses while you're at it."

Happy to have an excuse to escape, I said, "Fine."

The historical society decorated each of the tour houses with red, white and blue bunting, which in our case helped conceal the peeling paint and neglected garden. Billy's pick-up was parked in his mother's driveway, but he and his shirtless torso were nowhere in sight. I was unsure whether I was relieved or disappointed. He hadn't been around much lately, although between my hours at St. Francis and my disastrous trip to Levittown, neither had I.

The boathouse door was open and I filled the ice bucket and carried back a tray of glasses. When I entered the kitchen, Lisa dumped a jar of store brand salsa into a chipped bowl and shouted, "You have no napkins. People will be here any minute!"

I placed the ice and glasses on the counter. "Let me try the boathouse."

I was in the walk-in pantry when the boathouse's sliding glass door opened. I looked up.

"Hey, Ellen. What're you looking for?"

"Napkins."

"I think I took them on the boat," my uncle Paul said as he reached into the fridge for a six pack of beer. "Come on, let's get them." Paul, with his goofy fishing hat and baggy shorts, looked much younger than his fifty years.

"You're not really going fishing, are you?" I asked as we walked to his new sailboat. Fiberglass and over fifty feet, it was a great improvement over the ramshackle wooden rowboats we used as kids. In the past few weeks Paul had softened towards me and seemed to have forgiven me for not coming home last Christmas, and the Christmas before that. I was relieved since, aside from Kitty, I'd felt closest to Paul growing up. Only seven years my senior, Paul was more of a brother to me than an uncle and I knew he felt closer to me than to Danny. Although Paul was a popular athlete at our local high school and ran with the "cool" crowd, he'd always tolerated me following him around like a puppy dog. Unfortunately, we'd grown apart over the years as a result of my move to D.C. and my feelings towards Lisa. If my mother's illness accomplished one good thing, it had brought us closer. If I could only hold my tongue and not tell Lisa to fuck off for the next few weeks, then this closeness had a chance of becoming permanent.

He smiled. "Of course I am."

"But what about the tour? Lisa seems to think that you have a meeting this afternoon."

He laughed. "Yeah, I have a meeting with some fish." Paul climbed onto the boat, held out his hand and pulled me aboard. I went below deck to the small kitchen area, and just as I found a damp pile of napkins, the boat lurched away from the dock.

"Hey, what's going on? Lisa will have a fit if I don't bring back these napkins."

"Lisa will have a fit anyway," he shouted over the boat's motor. "Besides, I need a fishing buddy and you haven't come out with me since you've been back."

A small rowboat manned by two teenage boys bobbed in our wake as we tore away from the Centershore bridge out toward the Sound. As we moved further from the shore, the heavy sour air of low tide was replaced by a cool breeze. I sat down and stretched my hand over the side. The roiling water splashed my arms and face.

Paul settled on a small cove just east of Northport harbor and dropped anchor. "It's a little late in the day, but I sometimes have luck over here. Want a beer?"

I squinted in the now hot afternoon sun. "Sure."

Paul handed me a beer before he began his ritual of baiting the hook and casting off. I'd seen him do this a hundred times, so I looked out onto the water and savored the view and the beer. Once his rod was settled into its holder, Paul sat next to and tapped his bottle against mine. "Cheers. Here's to successfully avoiding yet another house tour."

"I'll drink to that. Although, I'm not sure how you define success since I'm sure I'll get an earful when I get back. Lisa might even call Molly so it can be a two-prong attack."

"Oh, Lisa'll be fine and Molly, well, I thought she had thawed a little towards you."

"Little being the key phrase. No, I guess that's not fair. She's trying. And she did finally identify Mr. Mystery."

Paul almost dropped his beer. "What? She knows who your father is? I don't believe it."

"Believe it. My father was in the police academy with Bobby Connelly and later they were partners. Molly and Bobby even went to his wedding."

"Wait a minute, this guy knew all this time that he had a kid and never came to see you?"

"No, that's the strange thing. He didn't know I existed until I went to see him last week." I took another swig and finished the beer. "You want another one?"

"Yeah, but let me get it." Paul reached into the cooler, expertly opened the bottles and handed one to me. "I can't believe you met him. So what's his name? Where does he live?"

"Name's Denis Lenihan and he lives in Levittown."

"Jesus, El. Remember we used to pretend he was an astronaut? I can't believe he was a cop from Long Island, although I guess being a cop is kind of exciting. So what's he like? Is he a hard ass like Uncle Bobby was?"

The sun came out from behind the clouds. Whether from the heat or the conversation, my forehead was slick with sweat. I held the cold bottle against my head for a moment. "Broken is probably the best word I can use to describe him."

"Broken? What does that mean?"

"Just that, broken. His wife died last year, two of his kids don't really talk to him. He says he was a heavy drinker, an alcoholic really. He just stopped drinking this year."

Paul looked like he unsure what to say. "Well, that's good El, that he stopped drinking."

"Yeah, I guess it is for him." I stared out into the horizon.

"So what now?"

"Nothing." I didn't meet Paul's eyes. "He doesn't want to see me again."

"No, Ellie, that can't be. Why wouldn't he want to have you for a daughter?"

"He says he can't. It would upset his kids."

"Oh, Ellie." Paul gathered me in his arms. "It's his loss, sweetheart. It's his loss."

The stress of the last few months caught up with me and I began to cry. Paul stroked my hair while various fish stole his bait. We sat together for at least twenty minutes until I was all cried out.

"Feel better?" Paul wiped away my tears with a rough paper towel as if I was his ten year old daughter Kathleen and not a forty-three year old woman.

"I think so. I'd better clean myself up." I splashed metallic smelling water from the small bathroom below deck on my splotched face. When I returned, Paul had already re-baited the hooks and had the rods set up.

"You still up for a little fishing, or do you want to head back?" Paul asked.

"No, I don't want to go back. I don't think I can face the tour people yet."

"Yeah, me neither. Another beer?"

I smiled. "No. It seems to make me cry."

"Ellie, if anyone had an excuse to cry it's you. I can't believe that bastard had the nerve to turn you away."

"It's not really his fault, Paul. He didn't even remember meeting Mom."

"What do you mean?"

"It wasn't some great love affair like you and I imagined as kids. More like a one night stand."

"A one night stand?" Paul shook his head. "No, that can't be right. Not Rose."

"Well, you were around when she got pregnant. Do you remember her dating or even going out."

"Not really. But, I was only seven and Kitty always sent me to bed by eight o'clock so how the hell would I know."

"What do you remember, Paul? About Rose around that time."

He paused for a moment. "Well, I remember driving with my mother to pick her up from the convent, after my dad got sick. She wouldn't talk to us all the way home. I remember her making me peanut butter sandwiches for lunch and I remember standing with her on Centershore bridge and throwing stale bread to the swans. I don't know I remember random stuff, you know, kid stuff."

I swallowed hard and then asked him, "What about your dad, what do you remember about your dad?"

Paul stiffened. "Why do you want to hear about my father? You never asked about him before."

"It's something Mom said in her sleep a few weeks ago. She was really frightened when she saw Danny. She thought he was your father."

"Frightened? Why would she be frightened of a bedridden man?"

"I don't know, but he wasn't always bedridden, right? I think she was remembering something from before. When she was younger. Listen. Paul, just humor me. What do you remember about your father?"

Paul took off his hat and scratched his bald head. The carefree fisherman who'd kidnapped me from the dock had been replaced by this pensive man. "Mostly I remember being scared of him. I don't know why, I mean, he couldn't talk or really move. He would just grunt and drool a little. But those eyes. He would stare at me with those eyes." Paul looked away for a moment. "I almost never went in to see him. I'd only go in if Rose told me to bring something in to him. And, God forgive me, I'd race out of that room as soon as I could. That's something I've always felt bad about as an adult. That I didn't spend time with him and allowed him to rot away in that room, alone."

"But what about before he got sick. Were you afraid of him then?"

"I always remember being a little nervous around him. Danny says he was a severe sort of man. Very exacting. Always expected us to behave perfectly. I can't really remember much, but I do remember that. That nervous feeling when he inspected us on Sunday mornings before we went to church."

"Don't get mad at me but I have to ask you, did he ever hit you?"

Paul straitened up. "No. Never. I'd have remembered that."

"What about Danny? Do you think he hit him?"

"I don't think he so. Danny never said anything."

"Okay, I'm sorry for asking all of this. I'm trying to make sense of Rose's nightmare."

"El, that's probably all it was, a nightmare. Besides, she's not exactly thinking straight now, is she?"

"I know, I know. It was probably nothing, but do you ever remember any strange noises at night? Before your dad had his stroke."

"I don't know." He rubbed his temple for a few moments. He then looked at me and said, "I used to hear a banging, late at night. It was a thumping, really. I asked my mother about it once and she told me it was just the raccoons at the garbage. I remember thinking that it didn't sound like the thumping came from outside, more like it came from the house. But I didn't ask her anything else, and then whenever I heard it, I'd just turn over. Jesus, Ellen, I was a child. Maybe it was a raccoon."

"Yeah, you're probably right. Listen, I'm sorry to bring all of this up. I'm trying to process all of this. How my ex-nun mother who never left the house all of a sudden decided to hook up with a drunk policeman and produce me. What motivated her? Who is she, Paul? I swear, I have no idea who either of my parents really are."

Paul patted my hand. "She was a kid herself. She made a mistake, that's all."

"But, it's so out of character. It doesn't make sense."

"She loved you. Kitty adored you, and so did your two goofy uncles." Paul smiled. "That's all that matters. Who cares about the drunk cop? You don't need someone like him in your life now. You have your husband, your kids."

"I know, Paul, I know. It's just that I don't have much time left with Mom, and I would like to understand. Sister Elizabeth told me that if I had any questions for her, I should ask them soon. Before she loses the capacity to answer them."

"Hell, I don't know." Paul swallowed the last of his beer. "Maybe you should let it go. She's awfully sick, and well, shouldn't we just let her die in peace?"

"But, maybe she's not a peace. You didn't see her that night. She was pretty upset and she's been agitated a few other nights as well. Maybe she needs to talk about her past, in order to be at peace."

Paul shook his head. "I think that's just the tumors talking, not her past."

"Maybe." One of the rods bent toward the water. "I think you've got a bite there, Paul."

Later, after we unloaded the boat, Paul went into the boathouse to gut and clean the two fish he caught. I slowly walked back to the house and stepped aside as an elderly couple who were part of the house tour walked carefully down the stone steps from the garden.

As I climbed the steps to the garden, a car door slammed. I looked over to the Conroys. Billy's pickup rumbled as he started it. I caught Billy's eye and smiled. He nodded his head in acknowledgement as he backed down the narrow driveway and then drove past. I tried not to be hurt by his lukewarm greeting; there was only so much male rejection my poor brain could process at once. I continued up the steps, opened the screen door and prepared myself for Lisa's inevitable litany of complaints.

Chapter 15

Rose

I stared at Danny's nodding head and fought the effects of the sleeping pill. It seemed as if someone was always trying to knock me out. I knew they only wanted to alleviate my pain, but why, why did they make me sleep away the precious time I had left? I'll be sleeping long enough.

Sister Elizabeth stood in the doorway. "Rose, are you okay? Do you need another shot?"

"I'm fine. Just thinking."

She took the chair nearest my bed. "Is something bothering you?"

"Besides, dying?" I gave her a weak smile. "No, Lizzie, nothing in particular. I was thinking about my stepfather. The older Danny gets, the more he looks like him. It's scary, really."

"Scary?"

"Maybe that's not the right word. Uncanny? Is that better?"

"Rose, you shouldn't think about him. You did the best you could for him. He was a very sick man."

"He was sick," I said. A sick bastard, I added silently.

"Do you want me to sit with you until you fall asleep?" Elizabeth asked, the eyes practically falling out of her head. It was almost nine, and I knew Lizzie had been here since this morning.

"No, that's all right. I have sleeping beauty here in case I need him."

"All right. I won't be here tomorrow but I'll be back on Friday." She bent down and kissed my cheek. "Good night and God bless."

Danny stirred slightly as Lizzie closed the door, his head tilted back, a small line of drool dripped from his open mouth. I remembered standing in the doorway of Peter's downstairs bedroom. His eyes, so full of anger and hate, stared at me and wordlessly commanded me to wipe the spittle from his sunken face.

I remembered the front door banged, followed by the heavy clatter of Kitty's high heeled shoes. The noise woke my sleeping child. I suppressed a curse as I wiped Peter's battered face.

"The child's crying, love. She sounds hungry," Kitty called from the adjoining kitchen.

"I fed her an hour ago. You woke her."

My mother stood in the doorway to Peter's room beside the kitchen. "I don't know, she sounds hungry to me. Don't bother with him now, mind your child. Isn't it wonderful, Peter, how our little Rosie has her own baba now. Oh, I know if you could you'd offer her your congratulations, wouldn't you now, Peter?" Kitty said in the tauntingly sweet sing-song she used whenever she addressed the lump in the bed. Peter's eyes glowed with anger and he gurgled in reply.

"Sure, Peter, don't tire yourself now. We know you're happy for Rosie," Kitty said. "A baby is a blessing no matter what side of the blanket it's born on, don't you agree, Peter? Oh, Mrs. Hennessy had a few things to say about it, but I straightened her out, didn't I, Rosie?"

I said nothing as Peter's face reddened with temper. Kitty turned to me. "That child won't feed herself. Go give her a bottle and I'll feed this fella lunch. It is time for his lunch, isn't it?"

Surprised, I said, "Yes." In the two years I'd tended to Peter, I could probably count on one hand the number of times Kitty so much as touched him, never mind spoon fed him. But I supposed she could see how worn out I was by caring for a colicky infant. "There's chicken soup on the stove."

"Fine, love. Leave it to me."

Ellen drank half a bottle for me and after I rocked her for twenty minutes, she finally went to sleep. I laid down myself on my hard single bed, but was so overtired I couldn't sleep. I went downstairs to make myself a cup of tea. While I sat at the kitchen table, a horrible hacking sound came from Peter's room.

"Goodness, Peter, what is happening? Are you all right, love? You know, those old bats I used to nurse made that sound when they were choking. I used to turn them onto their side. I wonder if I should do that now, Peter, what do ya think? Aw, I'm an awful eejit, aren't I though. I can't really remember what I'm suppose to do.

94

Stupid cow, isn't that what you called me, Peter, back when you could talk? Stupid cow. I am an awful stupid cow, aren't I?"

I stood outside Peter's doorway. My mother stood by the window, Peter half sat up on the bed. His face was almost purple.

"I couldn't find water in a well, isn't that what you always said, Peter?" my mother asked, almost casually, as she continued to stare out the window. "Stupid bitch couldn't find water in a well. But you're right of course, Peter. I am very stupid. So stupid that I can't remember how to stop someone from choking. So stupid." She turned around to face Peter and didn't seem to notice me in the doorway. "Holy Mother of God, you don't look so good. Would you like me to call the doctor, Peter? Should I call the doctor? What's that number again? Let me see. I can't seem to remember. I'd better go check the phone book. Now don't you worry, Peter, I'll find that number."

The hacking from the bed slowed. Peter's eyes, filled with panic, begged me to help him. "Mama?"

"Oh, Rosie, not to worry, I have everything under control." Kitty brushed past me and headed to the phone.

I followed her into the kitchen. "Mama, I don't think he can breathe."

"That's why I'm calling the doctor."

"But.."

"I think the baby's crying." She flipped through the address book.

"But shouldn't we..."

Kitty grabbed my arm. "Rose, go tend to your child. Now."

I turned and looked at Peter's discolored face, his bulging eyes. Mother Superior's words rang in my ears: "Imagine you are caring for Jesus." I looked at Peter one more time before I turned and walked upstairs.

Danny's book fell to the floor with a thump and roused me from my thoughts. Danny jumped in the chair. "Rose? Rose, you all right?"

"Yes, yes I'm fine. I was dozing."

He walked over to me and peered into my face. "Then why are you crying?"

95

Chapter 16

Rose

"Oh no, Molly. How could you?"

Molly bit her lip. "She found a picture. What else could I do?"

I shook with temper. "Tell her you couldn't remember. Lie. Anything!"

"Don't you think I would have lied to her if I could? Ellen's not stupid. The resemblance was too strong. I had to tell her." Molly stroked my arm. She stared at me for a moment and then said hesitantly, "But that's not the worst of it."

"Mother of God, what else?"

"She drove to his house last week."

I was silent then. I'd spent years deflecting Ellen's periodic questions about her father. I couldn't even remember the last time she'd mentioned him. Why? Why now?

"Rose," Molly said, "believe me, the last thing I want to do is upset you and I wasn't even sure I was going to tell you. But, I want you to be prepared."

"Prepared for what?"

"For Ellen's questions. Apparently, the visit did not go well. I only got this second hand from Paul, but Denis doesn't want anything to do with her. Paul said she's upset, and you know how Ellen can be. If she brings it up, or starts attacking you the way she does, I want you to be prepared. And if it's too much for you, I can make sure that you're never left alone with her."

"I don't need to be protected from my own daughter," I snapped.

Molly sighed. "Rosie, it's me you're talking to. I know how Ellen is. I know how she treats you."

In as strong a voice I could manage, I said, "She's been excellent daughter. She's dropped everything to be with me. And we haven't fought once."

"I know," Molly said in a more conciliatory voice. "She's been wonderful. And I want her to continue being wonderful."

"This is all your fault!" I shouted, close to tears. "You've ruined everything! Just get out. I want to be alone."

"Calm down."

"Oh sweet Jesus, can I not have ten minutes to myself? Leave me alone, Molly. I mean it."

Molly, her face mottled with emotion, walked out and closed the door behind her.

My throat parched from the unaccustomed shouting, I reached over to get a glass of water. I silently cursed as my now unreliable hand knocked the glass from the bedside table. I hoped that the crash wouldn't bring Molly or an attendant into my room; I needed a few minutes alone. I'd had a solitary life, especially since my mother died, and all this constant company drained me. The small talk drove me mad. At least twenty times a day someone asked me if I was all right. I had terminal brain cancer. The daughter I adored was in a constant state of agitation or anger. I had some hard things to say to her, things I hadn't had the courage to say for the last forty years, and now I was running out of time. So no, I felt like telling them, I wasn't all right.

But of course I never said this. I'd say "I'm fine." Fine. I'd tell the teachers who eyed my constant bruises that I was fine, just clumsy. I told my aunt my first few months home from the convent that I was fine, that I didn't mind nursing Peter. I told my mother when I was suffering from morning sickness that I was fine, that I must've of caught a stomach virus.

Fine. I should have "she was fine" engraved on my tombstone.

Molly forgot to lower the shade and the afternoon sun filled the room and hurt my eyes. The small gnawing pain that this morning's demerol shot had made manageable, had grown in intensity. I hadn't asked for another shot; Ellen was due this afternoon and I needed to remain lucid.

Oh, how I longed for one of my mother's hot toddy's. Whenever I had a cold, she'd wrap me in the old quilt her mother sent from Ireland and make me a hot toddy with the Irish whiskey she hid from Peter. How I loved the soft oblivion it provided. The world was a safe place as I drifted off while my mother stroked my hair. Until that St. Patrick's Day in 1966, Kitty's hot toddies and communion wine were the only alcohol that had ever passed my lips.

St. Patrick's Day. I almost didn't make it to Brooklyn that night, but at seventeen Molly was too young to be let out on her own. Molly badgered her own mother for a month to be allowed to attend the St. Patrick's Day party her older boyfriend was throwing with his fellow police cadets. Auntie Margaret told Molly that either her father would accompany her to the party or me. Margaret always viewed me as a steady sort and thought I could be trusted to chaperone her flighty young daughter.

Kitty sulked about having to miss the Irish American Society's annual St. Patrick's Day dance, but Margaret must have piled on the guilt in order for Mama to grant me a weekend pass. While I wasn't particularly excited about spending an evening peeling young men off of Molly, I was happy to escape Rose Hill, if only for a few days.

"Is that all you brought with you?" Molly asked, slightly horrified as I carefully laid out a navy blue skirt and white cotton blouse on her bed. "We're going to a party, not a funeral."

I tried not to be too insulted; Molly was not known for her tact. "That's all I have," I said simply. I didn't tell her that it was my best outfit.

"Rosie, you can't look like Sister Mary Miserable tonight. Bobby will think I'm a big baby if he thinks my mother sent you along to watch me. You need to look like a girl who wants to have some fun. You know what I mean?"

I laughed. "Not really."

Molly dug through her overstuffed closet and pulled out a pink, form fitting dress. "Mom bought me this dress last week. I think it'll look great on you; we'll just need to pin it. And can I do your makeup and hair? Please?"

"Sure, but don't make me look like a clown."

"I'll make you look beautiful. You'll see."

While she didn't succeed in making me look beautiful, but she certainly made me look different. Auntie Margaret almost fell into her cup of tea when the two of us came down to the kitchen.

"Molly, what have you done to my poor niece?"

"Oh, don't listen to her, Rosie. If it was up to her we'd be wearing saddle shoes and poodle skirts!"

Auntie Margaret admitted defeat and said, "Have a good time you two, but be home by eleven. Don't make me send your father down after you."

I winked at Auntie Margaret as Molly rushed me out the door. While we walked the five blocks to Lenihan's Pub on Third Avenue, Molly filled me in on her six month romance with Bobby Connelly. Molly chattered on about Bobby and I listened, amazed by how different my cousin's life was from my own. She spent her days passing notes in biology class and giggling on the phone while I made dinner and changed bedpans. I wasn't jealous of Molly's life as much as I felt far removed from it. I'd graduated from high school less than three years earlier and yet I felt a million years older than pretty Molly.

My Uncle John had said at dinner that Lenihan's was usually a real old timer's bar. However tonight, except for the proprietor, Donal Lenihan, who stood behind the bar like an old crow, there wasn't a soul in the pub over the age of twenty-five. The cadets, many of whom had marched in the parade in Manhattan, were proudly decked out in their dark gray uniforms. Men outnumbered the women by at least three to one so we were greeted by loud cheers and catcalls when we entered the crowded pub. Drunk cadets swarmed us until the brawny Bobby fought them off. With a proprietary arm around Molly, Bobby led us to the bar.

"Donal, three beers," Bobby shouted over the din.

I raised my eyebrows at Molly, but she hissed at me, "Just pretend to drink yours if you want. Don't embarrass me."

I didn't want to make a scene so I smiled and pretended to sip the warm sudsy beer. No one was looking at me anyway so it was easy enough to pour the unwanted beer onto the pub's sawdust floor. More and more young policemen and their heavily made up dates squeezed into Lenihan's. Tired of being jostled, I sidled my way past the boisterous cadets and found a relatively uncrowded corner. From there, I observed Molly and counted the number of drinks she had. Fortunately, Molly was more concerned with making sure her lipstick didn't smear than drinking the sour beer, so I didn't need to intervene.

For the next hour I stood quietly in my corner and drank in the scene. To see so many people my own age laughing and flirting was enjoyable after my many months of exile, even if I wasn't an active participant. No one bothered with me except for the occasional cadet who told me to smile or offered to refill my plastic cup with cheap beer. That was until a blonde cadet walked up to me with a tray of shot glasses.

The cadet handed me a shot glass filled to the brim. "It's not St. Paddy's Day without Irish whiskey."

"Oh, no thank you," I said primly.

"I know you were sent to babysit Molly. I don't think she wants to leave anytime soon, so here, take this. It'll help pass the time."

The young man had such an engaging smile I didn't have the heart to refuse him. I lifted the shot glass. "Cheers."

"Cheers, Molly's bodyguard." The young man drank his shot in one gulp. Not wanting to be outdone, I followed suit. The whiskey burned my throat and my eyes teared. I looked up to see if my new friend noticed, but he and his tray of spirits had already moved onto to the next group of revelers.

The next hour passed much as the last with more singing and drinking. Molly found me twice to accompany her to the ladies room, where my sole purpose was to tell her whether she had enough lipstick on. I warned her that we would need to leave soon, but she pretended not to hear me as she hurried back to Bobby. After each visit I returned to my dark corner and continued to observe the party. My blonde friend visited me again and pressed another whiskey on me. The second affected me more than the first and I soon swayed to the music.

The crowd eventually thinned. Feeling guilty after leaving me on my own for so long, Molly finally waived me over. Bobby found us two seats by the bar. Bobby was telling us boastful stories of his football playing days at neighboring Xavier High School when my blonde friend from earlier took the seat next to me. "Still on guard duty?"

I smiled. "Yes."

"Hey, Connelly, when're ya gonna let this lady go home and go to bed. She's been a good sport."

"Rosie's having a great time, aren't you, Rose?" Molly shot me a death stare. "She's doesn't want to go home yet."

"I don't want to go home yet," I parroted back to my new friend.

He laughed. "Well, in that case we'd better get you another one of those whiskey's that you like so much. Pop," he said to wizened old man behind the bar, "four whiskeys."

Molly was so grateful to be allowed to stay out a little later that she said nothing when her ex-nun cousin knocked back a whiskey like a pro. And she said nothing when the blonde cadet put his arm around me as the four of us got together for a photo.

When there were only a few stragglers left, the bartender threw a ring of keys at my friend. "It was your party, boyo, so you can lock up."

My friend caught the keys expertly, as if he'd done so a hundred times before. "Night, Pop."

"Night, Donal," Bobby said. Bobby turned to my new friend and said, "Hey, Denis, one more round before we go."

Denis hopped over the bar and poured us, along with the three remaining stragglers, another round of whiskey. Molly didn't even attempt to drink it, but I on the other hand swallowed it straight back.

"That's my girl, Rosie," Denis said.

I smiled. I wasn't sure at that point whether I was drunk or not, given that I'd never been drunk before, but I did feel a certain lightness, a looseness. The three stragglers soon left.

After he finished the whiskey, Bobby said, "I'd better walk these ladies home."

"Aw, you gonna leave me all alone?" Denis asked me.

I smiled at him.

"It's okay, Bobby. I can walk her home," Denis said.

Molly, eager to walk home alone with Bobby, said, "Okay, Rosie. I'll leave the side door open for you," and then quickly grabbed her coat and dragged Bobby out the door before I could change my mind.

Denis followed them to the door and locked it behind them. He then called over to me, "You like to dance, Rosie?" Without waiting for a reply he walked over to the jukebox, punched in a few buttons and a slow song, I couldn't remember which one, played. He then took my hand and we swayed to the music. After the song ended, he led me across the floor, toward the back of the bar. Through the fog of the alcohol, I thought clearly, "I can take this chance. I can do this."

In a back room littered with papers, he gently kissed me. I willed myself not to flinch as his hands explored my body over Molly's dress. As if in a dream, I soon found myself laying beneath him, naked, on an old couch, its upholstery torn and reeking of stale beer. His movements were smooth and well practiced. He barely seemed to notice when I cried out in pain.

When it was over, Denis rolled over on his side and almost instantly fell asleep. I listened to his drunken snores and laid there, still. When I thought enough time had passed, I climbed over Denis' almost lifeless body and got dressed. I felt slightly dizzy, from both the whiskey and the close, rank air of the room. The crisp air of the dark Brooklyn streets cooled my fevered skin as I walked the five blocks back to Auntie Margaret's. I crossed myself when I passed the Visitation convent, only two blocks from Margaret's house, and said a quick prayer in front of the statute of Our Lady. A prayer asking for forgiveness for my recent sin. A prayer that, nonetheless, God would grant me a blessing from that sin.

A cough from the corner of the room brought me back to my hospital bed, back to my current prison. I opened my eyes, and even without my glasses, saw the outline of my daughter.

"What time is it?" I asked, my voice rough from sleep.

"After one. Are you hungry? They brought by lunch a half hour ago, but I can ask them to bring you something."

I reached for my glasses and once they were on, Ellen came into focus. Her short, somewhat severe haircut had grown out a bit, and framed her face in soft blonde waves. Her eyes looked even bigger than normal in her thin face. Her mouth was a slash of red against her pale skin. In her hand she held something tightly. It looked like a piece of paper.

"What do you have there?"

Slowly, she made her way over to the bed and placed the paper into my hand. But it wasn't a piece of paper. It was a photo. An old, creased photo.

"I know," she said. "I found this and Molly told me. I've met him, Denis, and I've heard his side of the story. Now I want to hear yours."

I looked at the photo and smiled despite myself, to see me and Molly looking so young and pretty. "He was a handsome man, your father."

"Is that what happened, Mom? You were carried away, seduced by a handsome man?"

I laughed. "Hardly."

"Well, what then? Were you drunk?"

"I had been drinking, yes, but I wouldn't say I was drunk."

"Well, what then?" Ellen asked, her usual irritation with me seeping through. "Did he force you? Attack you? Rape you?"

"Goodness, no. Nothing like that. He was a lovely fellow, from what I can remember."

"Okay, well, if he was such a lovely fellow, then why didn't you contact him when you found out you were pregnant?"

"I never thought to."

"You never thought to? What do you mean you never thought to?"

"I just stayed home. I had responsibilities at home."

Ellen paced the room. "Why are we playing twenty questions here? Why can't you simply tell me what happened."

"Ellen, sit down. You're making me dizzy."

Ellen took her seat, and waited for me to continue.

"I met a man and got pregnant. Then I had the baby, you obviously, and raised you with my family. That's all that happened, Ellen. I don't know what else you want me to say."

"You can't honestly think that that is an acceptable answer. After all this time, that's it? That's the big reveal?"

I said nothing.

"Why did you, an ex-nun, have a one night stand with a guy you didn't even know? Why? What did you want? To experience sex, was that it?"

"You. I wanted you," I whispered. My head pounded and my vision blurred. "I'll tell you more tomorrow. Get the nurse, Ellen. Now."

Chapter 17

Ellen

Armed with a large coffee and bran muffin, I walked into my mother's room. The blinds were closed, so I quietly made my way to the chair in the corner without disturbing my mother's sleep. She'd been sleeping longer and longer these past few days.

About an hour later she opened her eyes. I handed my mother her glasses and helped her sit up.

"How long have you been here?"

"Not long," I answered. "I'll have them bring in your breakfast."

"Tell them just tea and toast. I can't face those eggs."

After my mother managed to eat her meager breakfast, she said, "Fire away."

"Fire away?"

"Yes. Fire away. Ask me the rest of your questions. Let's finish this."

My mother's cheeks seemed to have sunken even further overnight. I should forget all this, but of course I couldn't. "I've been thinking about what you said yesterday, about sleeping with Denis because you wanted a child, and it still doesn't make sense to me."

"Why? I would think you of all people would understand," my mother said without inflection.

I looked at her, surprised. My mother had never even seemed to notice that my twin boys were born only seven months after my hasty wedding, and she'd certainly never asked me about it.

"True, I was pregnant at my wedding, but I had a wedding. I got married and created a family. There was no groom in your scenario."

"You wanted a husband. I only wanted a child. Something of my own."

"Do you think it was fair to bring a child into the world without a father?"

"I don't know," she said with a somewhat confused look on her face, as if such a question never crossed her mind. "I think fathers are overrated."

Not exactly the answer I'd expected. I continued my interrogation. "But weren't you planning to go back to the convent after Peter died?"

"Of course I wanted to return to the convent, but the doctors said that Peter's heart was strong, that he could live for years. In my day, only young girls were allowed to enter the convent. I thought I'd be too old by the time Peter finally died."

"What do you mean? I thought he died when I was an infant."

She said nothing for a few moments. Then, without looking at me she said, "Yes, well, that was an accident. He choked."

I said slowly, "And then it was too late for you to go back, wasn't it? You were finally free to return to the convent, but you couldn't. Because of me."

She nodded slightly.

"If you hadn't gotten this 'something of your own' then you would've been free to leave that house and return to the convent."

My mother said nothing.

"But instead, you were stuck there. Is that right, Mom? Do I have that right?"

She looked at me unapologetically. "I always loved you, Ellen. I did the best I could for you."

"But you didn't want me. Once you finally realized what you had gotten yourself into, you didn't want me."

"I'll be honest with you, Ellen, I was young when you were conceived. Perhaps I acted rashly. I had some regrets, yes. But, that doesn't mean that I didn't love you."

Tears gathered in my eyes. "My father doesn't want me now. You didn't want me then. Kitty probably didn't want another child in her already overcrowded house."

Rose reached for my hand. "You're twisting my words around like you always do. You're not hearing me. I said I've always loved you. Kitty and my brothers loved you. You may not have had the perfect nuclear family, like the Conroys, like you created for your children, but you had a family that loved you. You have to believe that."

I snatched my hand from her. "I don't know what to believe anymore and I don't know why I even bothered coming back up here. For what? To sit by and watch the mother who resented me and lied to me my whole life? Denis was single when you got yourself pregnant. He seems like a decent guy. He probably would've done the right thing by you. Married you. Been my father."

My mother looked away from me and stared out the window for a few moments, and seemed to focus on the statue of the Blessed Virgin. Without looking at me, she said in a strange hollow voice, "I never would've married him, Ellen. I'd never marry any man. I wouldn't put myself through that, not for anyone. Not even for you."

Feeling slightly hysterical, I shouted. "Why? Because you're a lesbian? Is that it? Is that why you wanted to live with a bunch of women?"

My mother finally faced me. "I'm not a lesbian, Ellen," she said, without rancor. "I wanted to devote myself to God. That's why I joined the convent. After seeing my mother's marriage to Peter, I never wanted to get married myself."

"I don't know what to believe. What if this is another one of your lies or half truths?"

My mother deflated before my eyes. She pulled the covers up to her chin. "I don't know what else I can say to you. Maybe you had better leave."

"Yes," Molly said from the doorway. "I'll stay here with Rose. Ellen, why don't you go home and collect yourself."

"Fine, I'll leave. And I might not come back." I grabbed my purse and pushed past Molly.

Roaring out of the parking lot, I nearly mowed down poor Sister Elizabeth as she pushed one of the residents in a wheelchair. Too angry to stop and apologize, I continued my frenzied ride home. Once there, in the hot, stuffy house, I paced the rooms and randomly rifled through drawers and searched for what, I didn't know. More clues. More answers. What was this family that I was thrust into and what other secrets did these old walls hide?

But, my search turned up nothing. A gas bill from 1982. Kitty's expired passport. Paul and Lisa's wedding invitation. Just meaningless bits and pieces. Nothing to tell me who my mother was. Who I was.

After an hour and nearly faint from the hunger, I went to the kitchen. All I could find was a solitary almost expired yogurt and half a loaf of stale bread. I made a cup of strong tea, took two aspirin and ate the yogurt. It was only eleven and without my St. Francis duties I was at loose ends. I tried to catch up on a few emails, but the letters seemed to float around the screen and I couldn't make sense of them. I finally snapped the laptop shut, took the stale bread from the counter and walked out the front door without locking it. I walked across the road to the Centershore bridge. Whenever tensions between my grandmother and mother ran too high, I would always escape to the bridge. My grandmother used to gently scold me for wasting her fine bread on the swans and ducks, but on some level she realized that the breeze and the waves were my refuge.

I swung my legs over the side of the railing, tore the bread and dropped the pieces aimlessly in the water to the delight of the eager diving fowl. My old haunt provided no solace, however, as the strong mid-day sun scorched my unprotected neck and shoulders. Lost in my own tangled thoughts, I barely registered the roar of the motorcycle.

"Don't do it!" Billy shouted from his motorcycle.

I spun around. "Don't do what?" I asked blankly.

"Jump. Don't jump."

"It's about three feet of water."

Billy turned off the bike and sat next to me. "It was a joke, Ellen." He then touched my face. "Hey, are you all right?"

"Am I all right? Well, let's see. I'm married to a philandering asshole. My children are grown and don't really need me anymore. My long lost father told me that he never wanted to hear from me again. My mother admitted that having me was a mistake and that I basically ruined her life. Oh, yeah, and I accused my sick, dying mother of being a closeted lesbian. So I don't know, Billy, what do you think?"

Billy smiled. "I think you need a ride."

"Oh, I thought that offer was rescinded."

"Not that kind of ride, you perv, A ride on my bike. After my dad died, the only thing that helped was getting on the road. Come on, hop on."

Billy's hair, longer and blonder since I'd last seen him, danced in the hot summer breeze. His muscles strained against his tight faded t-shirt. In an attempt to suppress a sudden wave of desire, I looked down at the water. "Don't you have to work?"

He gently lifted my chin to face him. "Yeah, but who cares. Let's go."

Without another word, I hopped on the back on the motorcycle, snuggled tight against his worn Levis and we roared off. This time Billy wasn't quite so careful and I clung to him tightly when he took a sharp curve. We soon hurtled down the Sagtikos Parkway. Billy expertly weaved between minivans while I held tight. We soon veered off the highway and raced along the backstreets of an unfamiliar South Shore town until he stopped in front of McKee's Waterside Tavern, a ramshackle pub facing the Great South Bay. Billy easily hopped off the bike and offered me his hand.

"I know it doesn't look like much," Billy said, somewhat apologetically, "but they have the best raw bar on the Island. You're not going to believe the oysters."

In vain, I ran my fingers through my hopelessly tangled hair. "Do they have alcohol? Because as long as they have alcohol, we should be fine."

Billy took my hand and led me around to the back of the pub, onto a large deck overlooking the bay. The deck was packed with bikers, boaters and a young family struggling to control toddler twin boys. I smiled as the harried mother, her dish-water blonde hair twisted in a messy ponytail, attempted to feed a chicken finger to the more recalcitrant twin.

The waitress led us to the table behind the young family. "That brings back memories."

"I don't know how you handled three kids. One just about killed me." Billy gallantly held out my chair.

"I don't know either, to tell you the truth. I think I was too young and stupid to be scared."

"Ellen, you're many things, but stupid is not one of them. Now, what do you want to drink?"

"Margarita, frozen, no salt," I said to the waitress who had appeared, "and keep 'em coming."

Billy order a beer and a selection of clams, oysters and shrimp. The sun, still strong, burned through the table's flimsy umbrella. I could almost feel the freckles erupt across my cheeks. While I'm sure I looked like a tomato, Billy stretched his legs out like a cat and his tawny skin drank up the sun.

After our second drink, Billy looked at me uncertainly and said, "So, do you want to talk about your mother."

I sighed. "Quite honestly, no. I've done nothing but think about my mother and our fucked-up relationship for weeks now, and I can't talk about it anymore. You know what I really would like to talk about, though, is why you stopped to say hello to me."

"Well, I felt sorry for you. You looked so sad sitting there on that bridge."

"Sorry for me? Wow, you sure know how to make a girl feel special."

Billy smiled then. He placed his hand on his heart and said dramatically, "I couldn't help myself. You looked so beautiful sitting there, with the sun cascading on your shoulders."

"Burning them to a crisp." I laughed. "Okay, okay, you don't have to tell me why you stopped. But I'm glad you did."

"Me too, Miss Murphy." He swigged his beer. "Me too."

Billy and I practically inhaled the oysters and clams, and then chased them with cold bottles of beer. Billy entertained me with stories of his failed love life: the blind date that tried to convert him to Mormonism, the nymphomaniac who was also his son's English teacher. As I laughed about his latest foray on internet dating, I caught the eye of the harried young mother. Her white t-shirt was embellished with ketchup and chocolate milk. Her eyes, shadowed with tiredness and something else. Envy perhaps? Through her sleep deprived eyes Billy and I must look like a relaxed older couple whose chocolate milk and fish stick days were long behind them. She probably envied me my renewed empty nest sex life with my sexy husband. Oh, honey, I thought, if you only knew.

A gust of wind blew the paper napkins from our table. I noticed the sky had clouded over.

"I don't like the look of those," Billy said, eyeing the ominous sky. "Let's get out of here before it starts to come down."

We'd almost made it back to the North Shore when the first fat drop landed on my bare shoulders. The roads were soon slick and Billy took the winding curve of the exit ramp slowly. He was about to turn onto Route 35 towards Centerport, when I shouted over the roar of the traffic, "Keep going straight."

Without answering me, Billy continued north, past the shopping malls and car dealerships until he reached the bucolic streets of Northport. The rain came down in sheets and the wind picked up and shook the ancient pine trees lining Billy's street. A burst of thunder exploded as Billy opened his front door. I involuntarily jumped. Billy flipped the light switch by the door but nothing happened.

"Damn it. The minute it rains I lose power. I'll get a flashlight."

I stood in the darkened doorway, wet and cold and wondering what the hell I was doing in Billy Conroy's house. Billy soon returned armed with a flashlight and two towels.

"You must be freezing. Why don't you take a hot shower," he commanded rather than asked. He took my hand. "This way."

Billy led me up a narrow stairway and into his bedroom. Unlike the rest of the house, which looked like a construction zone, this room appeared to be finished. Billy open a drawer and soon the room was softly lit with the light of several candles.

Billy handed me a candle and two towels. "The bathroom's in there. I'll find you some dry clothes."

I nodded and took the candle from him. The bathroom was large with a large soaking tub along with a shower. I quickly stripped off my wet t-shirt and shorts and entered the shower. Enveloped in streams of hot water spouting from the ceiling and jets along the wall, I laughed. I should have known that Billy would have a souped up shower.

I luxuriated in the shower and allowed the hot water to ease the sting of my burnt skin. After twenty minutes I forced myself to turn off the water. Wrapped in a towel, I walked into the bedroom to find Billy sitting on the bed. The calm from the hot shower immediately left me and I was soon nervous—I was nearly naked in the same room as the beautiful Billy. Billy held a small bottle and walked over to me. He squeezed something onto his hand and then gently smoothed it onto my shoulders. I shivered as Billy rubbed cool aloe along my shoulders and back. I was so numb with nerves that I barely registered the pain of the sunburn or the relief provided by Billy's soothing lotion. Billy then turned me to him and rubbed the aloe on my chest. His eyes glowed in the candlelight.

Billy's fingers grazed the top of my breast. His expression was inscrutable. No longer the helpful neighbor. No longer the cheerful childhood friend.

My breathing was shallow. He continued his soft movements, unwilling to take it any further without a sign from me. Almost against my will, I ran my hands through his damp hair and allowed my towel to fall to the floor. Billy then kissed me with a fire and intensity that both scared and excited me. I allowed him to push me onto the bed. He quickly striped off his t-shirt and exposed the rippled muscles I'd admired all summer. I helped him take off his jeans. A snake tattoo circled his hip. I was consumed with desire; desire for Billy and desire for the oblivion his body could provide.

In the soft candlelight it was as if Billy worshiped every square inch of my flesh. "You're so beautiful," he murmured, almost to himself. "I can't believe how beautiful you are." His words and touch washed over me and soothed my burnt body and tortured soul.

The next morning I awoke, alone and naked, entangled in Billy's sheets. The sun streamed in through a bay window. I should get up and go home, but the thought of facing my mother, Lisa, Molly, all of them, was too much. I ignored the late morning sun, buried my head in the pillow and fell back asleep.

The smell of strong coffee and the sound of sizzling bacon finally roused me. My stomach rumbled and I forced myself to get dressed in the t-shirt and sweatpants Billy left folded next to the bed. When I entered Billy's semi-habitable kitchen, he was hard at work at the small stove.

"Morning, Beautiful. Coffee's over there." He pointed to the counter.

"You made breakfast?" I asked, unable to hide my surprise. A man who catered to me rather than the other way round was an alien concept.

He smiled. "Well, it's after two, so I think it's officially brunch. It's nice out. The storm last night got rid of all the humidity so I thought we could eat on the deck."

"Perfect." I carried the plates and cutlery out onto the deck. A canopy of old elms protected the deck and my still raw skin from the afternoon sun. Billy made several trips in and out of the kitchen, carrying coffee, eggs, bagels, cream cheese, napkins. He refused to allow me to help, so I sat there, smiling, as Billy bustled about.

111

We ate in companionable silence, smiling shyly at each other. After brunch, Billy asked whether I wanted him to drive me home. My face fell. I wasn't ready to leave the safe cocoon of Billy's bachelor pad. But I didn't want to be a pest either so I said, in as nonchalant a tone as I could muster, "Sure, whenever you're ready."

Picking up on my mood, his hands circled my waist. "Hey, don't feel like I'm kicking you out of here. I'd keep you here all day if I could. I just thought, you know, with your mom and all that you'd need to get back."

Feeling bold, I kissed him long and hard. "Do I look like a woman who wants to leave?"

Without another word, we returned upstairs.

Several hours later, we finally emerged from the house. Hand in hand we walked to the village like a couple of teenagers. Billy and I were licking ice cream cones when two motorcycles roared by, a grizzled biker shouting "Way to go Billy."

"Oh no, am I ruining your tough biker image?"

"You could only improve my image, Ellie. Only improve it."

For the next two days Billy and I hid from the world. For the first time in years, I felt cared for and, dare I say it, loved. I refused to think about any of my responsibilities, not my mother, not my kids and most certainly not my husband. For once I didn't worry about what I was supposed to do, what I should do. I thought only about the heat between myself and this sweet but sexy man.

Billy got an emergency call from a work site so he finally had to leave the house without me. I amused myself by reading one of his science fiction novels, a strange tale involving a vampire and a space alien. Sitting out on the sheltered back deck, I was so caught up in the ridiculous book that I didn't hear Billy's car and was startled when he walked onto the deck. His face was serious and he didn't return my smile.

"What?" I asked. "What's wrong?"

He sat down in the lounge chair next to mine. "I heard from my mother. Apparently half of Rose Hill has been looking for you. Your sister-in-law, what's her name, Laura? Well, she found the front door to your house open, with your purse and keys inside. She called the police and I think they contacted your husband. They were about to drag the harbor. I'm sorry, sweetheart, but I called the police and told them that you were with me."

112

The door. I completely forgot that I left the door open. Poor Billy looked so worried. I rubbed his back. "Don't be sorry. It's not your fault. I'm the idiot who left the door open and ran away from my life."

"Well, I'm the idiot who kidnapped you."

I laughed. "Thank God you did, otherwise then maybe I really would've drowned myself in the harbor."

He smiled. "So you're not mad at me?"

"Never." I kissed him lightly. "Never."

"Do you want me to drop you at the house or St. Francis?"

"The house. I'm still not sure whether I'm going back to St. Francis."

Billy shook his head. "Come on, Ellen. You know you're going back."

I stood up and paced the deck. "I honestly don't see why I should. She never wanted me. I ruined her life. We've never gotten along. All we do is fight now. She's probably better off without me."

"She's your mother, and despite your differences, you need to be there for her."

"She has plenty of people there for her," I snapped. "Molly, my uncles, Sister Elizabeth. People who don't annoy her like I do."

Billy stopped me mid-pace and hugged me. He guided me to the lounge chair and took my hand. "You need to be there as much for you as for her. Look, in a few weeks she'll be up in the sky, sucking oranges or whatever it is that people do in heaven. And where will you be? Down here with a suitcase full of regrets, and if you're not careful you'll be lugging that luggage around for the rest of your life. Believe me, I know what you're going through. When my father was dying, I had to deal with the two wonder brothers who could do no wrong in my parents' eyes. They would swoop in from their important jobs, tell me what I was doing wrong and then swoop out again. I was left to do all the dirty work. Holding my father's hand as he threw up, mowing the lawn, carting my mother back and forth to St. Francis when she was too shaky to drive. But, who did my father listen to and respect? My brothers. Not me. I was tempted, sorely tempted, to just give up. But I didn't. And now I can say I have no regrets."

"Well, maybe you're just a better person than me."

"Hardly. Look, I think we have something real starting here. I don't know where it's going to take us. Maybe I'm being selfish, but things will go smoother with us if you're not wracked with guilt about your mother. And if you don't go back there and make peace with her, that's exactly what's going to happen."

"So this is about you wanting to date Miss Happy?"

"Yes, that's what this is about." He kissed me gently. "No really, Ellen, you know I'm right."

I pushed a stand of hair behind his ears. I sighed. "I know. Okay, I'll be a big girl. I'll go back to St. Francis. But, drop me off at home first. I can't spend another day in these clothes."

"There's my girl. You won't regret it, sweetheart. I promise."

Twenty minutes later, Billy and I pulled up in front of my mother's house. Brendan's car was in the driveway and my wayward husband sat on the porch.

"You going to be okay?" Billy asked as he helped me off the bike. "Do you want me to stay?"

"No, I'll be fine," I said in a confident voice, despite the flutters in my stomach. "I'll call you later."

He squeezed my hand. "You'd better."

With as much dignity as I could muster, I walked up the steps. I adopted an airy, carefree tone. "Hello, Brendan. I didn't expect to see you back here."

"The police called and told me that you'd disappeared. I'm in the middle of the biggest case in my career and I had to drop everything to come here. We all thought you'd been abducted or drowned. Your cousin Molly was a wreck. And you're off riding motorcycles and doing God knows what with the gardener?"

"He's not a gardener."

"I don't care what he is!" Brendan shouted. "All I know if that I had to interrupt what I was doing to come down here!"

I could probably count on one hand the number of times Brendan has raised his voice to me. Benign neglect was more his style. Three months ago, I would've coddled him at the slightest sign of anger, but not now. I opened the front door. "Well, as you can see," I said lightly, "I'm fine so you can go back home to your very important life."

"Don't you dare walk away from me! Is that all you have to say?"

114

"Yes, Brendan. That's all I have to say. Now if you'll excuse me, I need to take a shower before I go see my mother."

I didn't make it beyond the hallway before he grabbed my arm. "What has gotten into you? Do you have any idea how much trouble you've caused me? I've had to pick up the slack at home while you've been up here playing house with Mr. Motorcycle."

I stepped away from him and laughed. "Slack? What slack have you taken up?"

"Well, I had to take care of the kids."

"Take care of the kids? Our children who are in college? Okay, tell me, Brendan. What exactly have you done to take care of the kids?"

"I had to send the boys money. And I had to pick Veronica up from the airport last week."

"By pick up do you mean arrange for a car to pick her up?"

"Well, yes," he said defensively, "but that's more than you did."

"You've got to be kidding me. I've cared for those children for close to twenty years. I've cared for you and our home and you're bitching because you had to write a few checks and tell you secretary to call a car service?"

"That's not the point. It's not my job, it's yours."

"Well, maybe I don't want that job anymore. Maybe I quit."

"Why?" Brendan snarled. "So you can play house with the loser next door?"

"Careful, Brendan," I said over my shoulder as I walked into the kitchen. "You almost sound like a jealous husband. Like a husband who cares."

He followed me. "Of course I care, Ellen. I love you."

"You love me? Is that why you've ignored me and cheated on me for twenty years?"

"I never..."

I leaned against the countertop. "Oh stop it, Brendan. Don't insult my intelligence. I've seen you. I've seen you walk into hotel rooms with those bimbos. Some of them have even called me, crying, after you dumped them."

Changing tack, Brendan said, "I'll admit that I've had some relationships. But that's because you moved me out of the bedroom. I'm a man. What did you expect me to do?"

115

"The cheating started long before that and you know it."

"I gave you everything you wanted. A beautiful home, money, the kids. I married you when you got knocked up. I held up my end of the bargain."

"Maybe you did, Brendan. But maybe now I want to strike a new bargain."

"What are you talking about?"

I sighed. "Look, we can talk about this when I get home. My mother's dying. I have to focus on her now, not on our pathetic excuse for a marriage."

"Pathetic? Come on, our marriage isn't pathetic. We've had some laughs."

"Laughs?" I asked ruefully. "After twenty years you should be able to say something more than that, don't you think?"

Suddenly Brendan looked defeated. He looked old. "I don't know what you want me to say here, Ellen. I don't know what you want me to do."

"Go home," I said, almost gently. "I want you to go home."

When I came down from my shower, he'd gone.

Chapter 18

Rose

"Rose, I have a surprise for you," Molly said from the doorway.

"Ellen? Is Ellen here?" I asked hopefully.

"Well, no. Her cold is still very bad. But, I'm sure she'll come as soon as she can," Molly said unconvincingly.

"Oh." I slumped back onto the bed.

"What kind of greeting is that?" scolded a quivering brogue from the hallway.

"Auntie Maura! What are you doing here?"

Maura, her spine curled with osteoporosis, shuffled over to me. "Molly sprung me from Sunny Hills. Now, love, how are you holding up?"

Struggling to sit up I said, "I'm fine."

"Fine? Ah love, you're far from fine, God help you." Auntie Maura landed a dry kiss on my cheek. With effort, Auntie Maura settled herself in the chair while Molly looked on from the doorway. "Sure, my poor heart broke when I heard the news. I wanted to come sooner but Sean and Jimmy wouldn't let me come. And of course those witches they married were too busy to drive me over. It might interfere with their nail appointments. I tell you, girls," she said looking over to Molly, "you're lucky to have daughters." Turning back to me, she continued, "I know you've only the one, Rosie, but thank God you had a girl. You don't have to depend on the favors of other women's daughters." I smiled. Her stream of chatter was a comfort. Having married a fellow Irishman, Maura's brogue had never been diluted by her many decades in New York. It had been a long time since I heard the County Kerry accent; it reminded me of my mother.

"Ellen came up from Washington to stay with Rosie. She's been a godsend," Molly said, trying to sound sincere. "She'd be here only she's fighting a heavy cold."

"The poor thing. Well, Rosie, you're very lucky. Ellen was always such a beautiful girl. And smart. She's a credit to you, she is."

"Thank you, Maura."

"And the grandchildren? Tell me what they're up to?"

We chatted for the next half hour about our various grandchildren, and in Maura's case, her great-grandchildren. Auntie Maura, at eighty, was the sole surviving O'Connor sibling, and the de facto matriarch of our branch of the family. Aside from osteoporosis and a touch of arthritis, she was healthy as a horse. The only reason she was moved to Sunny Hills Assisted Living instead of one of her sons' homes was that neither daughter-in-law was willing to live with her sharp tongue. Molly and I both thought it was shameful that they stuck poor Maura in a home just because she spoke her mind.

I enjoyed my visit with Maura, although her wrinkled face and watery blue eyes were a sad reminder of what I would've eventually looked like had I not been cursed with this cancer. However, I soon tired. Maura seemed to sense this, so she sent Molly off to get her a cup of coffee.

Maura stroked my hand. "Now, love, they tell me that you're troubled. That you've been having bad dreams."

"It's nothing, Auntie Maura. Just the drugs they have me on."

"Well, I've been troubled ever since I heard your news." She was still for a moment and then grabbed my hand. "You know, Rosie, maybe I shouldn't say this now, but Margaret and I never felt right about letting you live with Peter. But sure, Kitty was your mother. She was within her rights to take you. But, we always felt bad. You have to know that."

I said nothing.

Undeterred, Maura continued. "I prayed for you every night, Rosie. I prayed that things were not as we suspected." Her eyes began to tear. "But they were, weren't they, love?"

I looking into her kind weathered face. "It doesn't matter now. It was so long ago."

"But, it weighs on me. I have to know, can you forgive me?"

"Auntie Maura, there's nothing to forgive."

"There is, child, there is. We should have tried harder with Kitty. Tried harder to get her away from him. But, she was my older sister and believe it or not I was easily bullied in my youth. Especially by Kitty."

My temples throbbed. "We don't need to talk about this. You shouldn't trouble yourself over this."

Her chin quivered. "But you are troubled, aren't you, Rosie?"

"I have nothing else to do but lie in this bed and think. Think about my life and the choices I made. I'll admit, I have thought about Peter these past few weeks. But what's done is done."

"So you forgive me?"

"Of course. Of course," I said faintly.

"Maybe you need to forgive your mother too."

Forgive my mother? For years my resentment of my mother was as much a part of me as my black hair and blue eyes. Some days it rose to the surface, such as when she and Ellen would giggle in the kitchen together as if I didn't exist. Other times, when Mama and I were in the garden, giggling together ourselves, less so. But, if I was honest, it was always there.

"Maybe," was all I said.

"She did her best. But she was proud, so proud. She couldn't admit she made a mistake. She loved you, Rose. She always loved you."

A flash then, flew across my mind. I could almost hear my mother tear into Mrs. Hennessy down the street when the nosy neighbor made a remark about my heavily pregnant belly. "I know."

"Look who I found," Molly announced from the doorway.

My Ellen stood behind Molly, her eyes soft, her skin pink from the sun. Ellen looked relaxed, almost happy. Nothing like the harridan who'd flown out of my room days earlier.

With effort, Maura rose from her chair and embraced Ellen. "Ah, love, you look lovely."

"You too, Auntie Maura." Ellen returned the embrace instead of standing there stiffly as she usually did. Ellen wasn't one for hugs. Even as a child, she'd squirm out of my arms.

They chatted briefly while I looked on and willed the creeping pain to stay at bay while my daughter was here. However my agony must have shown on my face because Molly left to call the nurse. Soon the nurse was shooing everyone out of the room while she attended to me.

"Mom, I'll just walk Maura out," Ellen said gently. "But I'll be back."

I nodded with relief.

Chapter 19

Ellen

I was beyond surprised when Molly greeted me in the hallway with a hearty, and seemingly sincere, hug. "Oh, thank God you're all right. You are all right, aren't you?"

"I'm fine, Molly. And I'm sorry..."

Molly rubbed my arm. "Not at all. So long as you're here now. That's what matters."

I couldn't believe my luck at avoiding a Molly smack-down. "Yes. I'm here now."

Molly led me by the hand into my mother's room, as if afraid that I'd disappear again. My mother's eyes were bright in her shrunken face as Auntie Maura patted the back of her hand reassuringly. When she saw me, my mother looked happy and relieved. Underneath my fake smile, I squirmed. My escapist romp with Billy while my mother was lying in her deathbed now seemed so selfish. Molly nattered on about my "cold" and Auntie Maura asked me how I was feeling as I walked her to Molly's car, but I knew my mother didn't buy it.

But luckily my mother's never been one to hold a grudge. She's also never been one to delve below the surface of any relationship, so we were both quite happy to gloss over my three day absence. Just as we have glossed over so much of our family's history. No more questions about Denis, no more questions about her aborted vocation. So much for closure.

The next week was calm, almost peaceful. My days were spent with my mother. I either watched her sleep or quietly chatted with her about nothing in particular: my children's preparations for college; the priest's sermon that was broadcast over the loudspeakers daily from the small chapel down the hall. My mother seemed calm and happy to have me near her. I bit my tongue about ten times a day but I continued the loving mother-daughter facade. Billy was right. I had to continue "doing the right thing" until the end. For my sake as much as hers.

Brendan called my mother's room twice over the week. Rose of course was delighted to hear from him. It gave her comfort to believe that my marriage was a happy one, my perfect little family intact. When I picked up the phone, he was his usual flirty, offhand self, as if our confrontation in the kitchen never happened. Like Rose, Brendan had decided to ignore my three day rendezvous.

But not Billy. Except for my two nights of Rose duty, we spent every night together in his Northport oasis. And I hadn't felt guilty about it. At least, not too guilty.

So things were going well, or as well as can be expected when you're conducting an illicit affair while your mother lays dying from terminal brain cancer. But I felt at peace finally; at peace with my mother and at peace with myself. I was a little late getting to St. Francis one morning—Billy and I had had a late night—when I ran into Sister Elizabeth in the hallway.

"Ellen! Aren't you looking marvelous?"

"I am?" I asked uncertainly.

"Yes. You look different somehow."

"I've gotten a little sun." And a little lovin' I left unsaid.

"Well, you look great." Despite her smile, her eyes were dead. Sister Elizabeth must have held the hand of hundreds of dying patients over her long career, yet it appeared that the death of her good friend was wearing on her. She gently touched my cheek. "I'm happy to see that you're holding up well. The next few weeks will be the hardest."

"You think she's near the end?"

"She's holding on, fighting it. But, it can't be much longer." Sister's smile faded. "She's in with the priest now."

"Why?"

"She asked to see him and make her last confession. He's been in there a while. They should be done soon."

The woman's been in her bed for the last six weeks. What on earth could she be confessing to? But I didn't say this to Sister Elizabeth. I simply told her I'd wait outside my mother's room until they were finished.

I arrived to find Molly pacing the hallway, the door to my mother's room slightly ajar. Although we all had assigned times to sit with my mother, Molly came at other times as well. We'd been getting along surprisingly well this past week. Given the circumstances, I think we both decided to cut the other some much needed slack. After we hugged hello Molly sat in the chair across from my mother's room while I took the one closest to my mother's door. I opened my bag to take out a book when the shouting started.

"I did it, Father. God help me I did it."

"Now, Miss Murphy, Rose, calm yourself."

"I will not calm myself. You're not listening to me. I've waited more than forty years to confess this. Don't you dare tell me I don't know what I'm saying. I know what I'm saying. I killed him. I killed my stepfather!"

I looked over at Molly, stunned. Molly rose from her chair and stood in the middle of the hallway, frozen, unsure what to do. I had no such hesitation. Disregarding the sanctity of the sacrament, I pushed the door open.

"You're a murderer? On top of everything else you're a murderer?"

My mother, turned to the priest and spat, "You pup! Didn't you close the door?"

The young foreign priest looked baffled.

I stood next to her bed. "Who are you? You killed your stepfather? Did you kill Kitty too? I suppose I should be grateful that I wasn't a victim of crib death."

"Ellen, no..." My mother reached for my hand.

I drew back my hand. "You pretend to be so holy, so good. You'd give me grief every time I missed mass. But you're a monster. A murdering, lying monster."

"Ellen." Molly grabbed my arm. "That's enough."

I spun around to face Molly. "Did you know about this?"

Molly wouldn't meet my eye.

"Fine. I'm done now anyway. I'm done with the lot of you!"

Chapter 20

Rose

    I walked through Peter's sparsely attended wake and then his funeral mass like a zombie. A few of the neighbors who didn't know any better tried to comfort me. They told me what a wonderful man Peter was, how respected the Frohllers were as one of the Centerport's founding families. I overheard one of the neighbors say to the other, "Look at how upset she is. He was such a good man, taking Kitty and Rose in. Treating Rose like his own daughter."

    The O'Connor sisters and their families were another matter. They did the right thing, they attended the wake, the funeral, the lunch after. They said, "sorry for your trouble" and shook our hands. But they didn't extol Peter's virtues as one normally would of the dead. They barely mentioned him at all.

    The house was calmer, lighter after Peter died. The boys brought their friends around and rough housed on the front lawn without fear of disturbing the invalid. Kitty was her normal, bubbly self. She ran the hardware store, fussed over baby Ellen and attended the Irish American Society's weekly dances. She slept sound at night. Her soft snores echoed through the upstairs hallway and mocked me as I suffered through yet another sleepless night.

    Two months after Peter died, Kitty and the boys fired up the ancient charcoal barbecue and cooked burgers and hot dogs. For April it was surprisingly warm, and we ate on the redwood picnic table in the backyard. Paul regaled us with stories of his latest baseball victory. Everyone was relaxed, smiling. We enjoyed the evening together. Like a normal family. Ellen, picked up on the mood and gave us all a toothless grin.

    For once the boys cleaned up without me nagging them and got themselves ready for bed without complaint. Ellen went down easily, her belly full of formula. My mother stood at the ancient stove when I walked into the kitchen.

    "A cup of tea, love?"

"Sure," I replied.

Kitty, usually the servee rather than the server, bustled about the kitchen and searched for a pair of cups with matching saucers. She carefully scalded the teapot before adding the loose tea leaves and hot water. She arranged a plate full of Italian cookies, as if she expected Barbara Conroy and her cronies rather than her bedraggled daughter. Kitty gave me a dazzling smile, poured me a cup of tea and made it just the way I liked it, light and sweet.

"Now, isn't this lovely. Just the two of us."

"Yes, just the two of us," I said blankly.

"Ah, love, drink your tea. Have a cookie. Cheer up for God's sake."

"Cheer up?"

"Anyone'd think you're the widow and not me," she said, still looking for a smile from me.

I resisted her charms. "I haven't slept in weeks."

Deliberately misunderstanding me, she said, "Well, sure, no young mother sleeps. I don't think I slept a full eight hours until you were two."

"No, Mama. Ellen isn't the one keeping me up."

With a forced laugh, Kitty said, "Don't tell me I'm snoring again. Danny always complains about my snoring but I refuse to believe it."

"It's not the snoring, Mama."

Her good humor now gone, she said, "Ah, I don't know what's got into you. We've had a lovely evening. But then, you always were a sour old thing."

Ignoring the insult, I said with conviction, "I'm going to confession tomorrow morning. I'm confessing to Monsignor O'Brien."

Mama took her half full tea cup to the sink and rinsed it out. "Sure, that's a great idea," she said over the roar of the faucet. "A good confession will set you right up."

With exasperation, I said, "I don't think you understand, Mama. I'm confessing."

"Sure, what else would you do in a confessional?"

I rose from my chair and shouted, "About Peter. About what we did to Peter!"

She spun around. "It was an accident."

In a small voice, I said, "Mama, for once can we not tell the truth? It was no accident."

"'Twas, love. You were so tired from caring for the child, you slept right through it. Isn't that what we told the doctor? He wrote it down on his certificate."

"Mama, please." The tears streamed down my face. "I can't live with this."

She handed me a paper towel for my tears. "There's nothing for you to confess to, Rosie. It was my fault. I should've been watching him but then I was busy in the garden and I couldn't hear him."

"Mama..."

"My fault, love," she said lightly. "My sin, not yours. But sure, accidents happen. Even the doctor said so. He said he sees it everyday. No one blames us, Rosie, no one."

"What about God?"

"The last one who would blame us is God."

In desperation, I cried, "I can't, Mama. I can't live with it."

Her eyes hardened then. "You'll have to, love. You have a child to raise. I have those two boys to educate. We don't have the luxury of indulging guilty consciences."

"I need to confess it."

"Then confess to the roses, confess to the trees, but for God's sake don't involve any priest in our business. Certainly not that fool O'Brien."

"Mama!"

"Ah, Rosie, you take all that religious malarkey too seriously. They're just men. They're not God. They're just men and we both know you can't always trust men, now can you?"

I sank into my chair. "I keep seeing his eyes, Mama. I keep seeing his eyes when I lay down at night."

Mama went to the cabinet and took out a pill box. She handed me a blue tablet. "Take one of these, Rosie, every night after dinner. You'll close your eyes and you won't see nothing, trust me. Take it." I obediently swallowed the pill and chased it down with my lukewarm tea.

"Now, there's my girl." Mama stroked my short hair. "There's my good girl."

For decades I'd confessed my spinster sins to Monsignor O'Brien and his successors at St. Ann's: losing my patience with my mother, my white lies to Lisa during family functions. I never confessed anything real. Not my lies of omission to my daughter. Not my other grave sin.

I finally gathered the courage to defy my mother's edict and asked Sister Elizabeth to arrange my confession with the young African priest. His English was marginal at best so hopefully he wouldn't ask me too many question. Maybe he wouldn't even understand me. Two Hail Mary's and then as my mother would say, "Bob's your uncle." Forty plus years of grief and guilt, poof. Gone.

Father Whats-his-name was a nice young man. His large dark eyes seemed kind. With care he carefully enunciated a prayer before I started my confession. My voice low and husky with emotion, I said, "Bless me Father, for I have sinned. It's been forty-two years since my last confession. My last real confession."

The priest's eyes got larger as I described for him in detail the bulge of Peter's eyes, the sound of my shoes on the old wood floor as I walked away from him.

In his hesitant English, he said, "Miss Murphy, you are confused. Let me get the doctor."

Forty years of anger and frustration poured out of me. "I've waited too long for this. I know what I'm saying. I killed him! I killed my stepfather!"

He tried to shush me, but I wouldn't be quiet. Over and over I shouted, "I killed him. I killed my stepfather!"

The door then flew open. Ellen's mouth moved but I couldn't make out what she said. It was if the world stopped. She came closer to me. She yelled at me. I opened my mouth but no sound came out. Ellen eventually stormed out.

The priest said nothing.

Molly, in tears, sat by my bed. "Why did you say that, Rosie? Why? Kitty told my mother that she's the one that let him choke to death. Not you. It's not your sin to confess."

"It is," I whispered. "It is."

Chapter 21

Ellen

My heels clicked along the tiled hallway, my eyes unseeing, blinded with tears. I plowed into an attendant carrying a tray of food, orange jello soon decorated the hallway and my shirt. I mumbled a sorry and then continued my march down the hallway. I was about to push open the glass doors to the parking lot when I heard a sweet high soprano. I stopped for a moment. Almost against my will, I followed the organ music to a small chapel. The chapel was dark, lit only by a few wavering candles and the weak afternoon sun that fought through the narrow stained glass windows. On the altar Sister Elizabeth sang the mass' entrance hymn, her voice surprisingly strong for a woman her age. A young African priest walked solemnly up the narrow aisle. Sister caught my eye and beckoned me to enter.

I sat among the half dozen members of the congregation and was silent. I didn't even mouth the refrains that, while I hadn't darkened the door of a church since my Granny's funeral, were still emblazoned on my brain. I sat with my tear-streaked face and jello-stained shirt and absorbed the lilting cadence of the priest's familiar words, my knuckles, white, as I held tightly to the well worn pew.

"...look not on our sins but on the faith of our Church..."

Look not on our sins. I wondered how God would look upon my mother's sins in a few weeks, or maybe even a few days, when they will presumably come face to face. Would forty years of manning the annual bake sale and decorating the altar outweigh a murder? What will she say? "Yes, Lord, I did have an illegitimate daughter and I did kill my stepfather, but how about those flower arrangements? What did you think of the lilacs? I grew them myself. Pretty impressive, huh?"

At least my mother had faith and service to counteract her sins. What did I have? What would He say to me? "I tricked my husband into marrying me, abandoned my mother on her deathbed and conducted a hot affair with my neighbor. Oh, but I used to be my daughter's Girl Scout leader." Somehow, I didn't think that would fly.

"For the residents of St. Francis," Sister Elizabeth said from her lectern. "That they find comfort for their pain and can find joy in the prospect of Heaven. Let us pray to the Lord."

"Lord hear our prayer," chanted the middle-aged couple sitting next to me.

"For the families." Sister Elizabeth stared at me. "That they find the strength to forgive, and the strength to love. Let us pray to the Lord."

"Lord, hear our prayer," I whispered.

Sister Elizabeth nodded slightly.

I began to get into the rhythm of the ritual. Sitting, kneeling, responding from some place within me that had been silent for a long time.

"Lamb of God, you take away the sins of the world. Have mercy on us.
Lamb of God, you take away the sins of the world, Have mercy on us.
Lamb of God, you take away the sins of the world. Grant us peace."

Peace? Was peace possible for the likes of me? For the likes of my mother?

The priest lifted the chalice above his head and calmly conducted the almost mundane mystery of transforming the bread and wine. I shook my head when Sister beckoned me up to the altar to receive this sustenance. She walked down from the altar, linked my arm and guided me up to the priest.

"The body of Christ."

"Amen." I opened my mouth.

I returned to me seat, knelt awkwardly, my hands clasped tightly together, my mind a blank. When I was young I always knew what to pray for: an A on a history test, a new dress for a party. To my childish mind, God was like a giant gum-ball machine in the sky. You plugged in the obligatory Our Father or Hail Mary and out came the requested treat. But God hadn't granted me my wishes for quite some time. I remembered sitting in Dahlgren chapel in Georgetown soon after Veronica's Holy Communion, begging Him to save my family. The little family that I worked so hard to create. I pleaded with Him to make my husband love me and honor me as he promised he would in that very chapel. I bargained with Him: I'll be a nicer to my mother, I'll attend mass every Sunday. But, as I found out when I followed Brendan and his blonde whore into the Four Seasons, God doesn't always answer our prayers.

But what should I pray for now? I knew I should ask for help, help in dealing with my constant anger. I knew I should beg for forgiveness for how I've treated my mother. Her sins didn't excuse my own. But, I was tired and I couldn't think. So I sat. Sat and listened to the tinny sound of the small organ and I let the music and the incense ease my frenzied mind.

After mass, Sister Elizabeth walked me to my car, still linking me as she would for one of the elderly residents.

"Allow Him to help you, Ellen. Allow Him to provide you with the strength and grace you need."

"Strength?" I fumbled through my bag searching for my keys.

"The strength to forgive your mother. The grace to forgive yourself."

I nodded mutely and climbed into my ostentatious car.

An hour later, I sat on the dock. My bare feet dangled over the side and skimmed the water. I shivered in the cool, almost autumnal afternoon breeze. Footsteps, hollow against the old dock's boards, roused me from my reverie.

She kicked off her white sandals and groaning slightly sat down next to me. "Damn arthritis."

I said nothing as I stared out into the harbor.

"He beat her," she said. "He beat the hell out of your mother. Your grandmother too."

"Please, Molly. I can't take much more today."

Molly ignored me and continued. "Kitty hid it. Denied it. But every time Rose came to my house she was covered in bruises. Broken fingers. Missing patches of hair. Kitty told my mother that Rose was just an active child, but Rose was timid. A bookworm. My mother never believed Kitty and neither did I."

I said nothing.

"He was a vile, nasty man. To hit a woman, a child. Who would do that?"

I finally turned to face her. "And that justifies murder?"

"Murder? Who even knows if there really was a murder. If Kitty and your mother really wanted him dead, why would they wait two years to do it? Your mother fed him, cleaned him, wiped his ass. I saw her with Peter. She cared for him tenderly, with kindness. More kindness than that bastard deserved. And she never complained, not once. I don't believe she murdered Peter. I don't."

"Well, then why did she say she did? She's told me so many half truths all my life that I don't know what to believe anymore."

"Misplaced guilt? I don't know, Ellen. I don't. But, at the end of the day, does any of this really matter? There are only three people who know what happened. Two are dead and one's about to be." Molly stroked my hair, as she would her young daughter. In a softer voice, she continued, " I think what you need to ask yourself is are you're really so horrified by her admission or are you just using this as an excuse not to deal with your mother, not to deal with her death."

"My head is spinning. I swear to God, Molly, my head is spinning with all of this."

Molly dug through her purse and produced a pack of cigarettes. She lit two and handed one to me.

"But I don't..."

"You do today."

We silently smoked our cigarettes. I choked mine down like a thirteen year old sneaking her first smoke; Molly with the relish of an unrepentant smoker. The sun was low in the sky and the midges had begun to bite, but neither one of us wanted to move. Molly stubbed out her cigarette and lit another. I slapped a mosquito.

"My mother died two months before my wedding. We fought over the seating chart the night before she died. A seating chart, can you believe it? But, I was only twenty-one, she was barely forty-five. Neither one of us dreamed that she wouldn't be there to dance at my wedding."

I said nothing.

"That might be one reason why I've never had patience for your attitude towards your mother. Look, I know it probably wasn't easy for you growing up in that house. I know things weren't perfect. But Rose loved you and she was there. She was there for your wedding. She was there when your children were born. She was there any time you needed her, any time you wanted her."

"I know."

"And now you have the opportunity to hold her hand as she dies. To be with her. You have no idea how much I envy you that. My mother died of an aneurism, alone in the bathroom. This time with your mother is a gift. Don't waste it." Molly stubbed out her cigarette, patted me on the back and awkwardly stood up. I watched her walk slowly back to the street.

I sat, almost frozen, on that dock for another hour. I didn't cry, didn't think, didn't pray. I just sat and allowed my limbs to be the mosquitos' dinner. I think I would've slept there if Billy hadn't found me. He lifted me up and led me like a child back to my mother's house.

Chapter 22

Rose

Monsignor Ryan held my hand as I made my confession. His deep Brooklyn baritone filled the room as he calmly granted me absolution. Only one Hail Mary and two Our Fathers to expiate my sins. We said the prayers together. After more than forty years, my soul was finally clear, whole. I now had God's forgiveness. At least I hoped I had God's forgiveness. I supposed I'd find out soon enough.

But, will I have my daughter's? I didn't know. I knew I didn't have much time left. The morphine drip I'd fought for so long was now permanently attached to my arm, pumping sweet relief into my veins. The jagged edge of pain kept at bay, along with hunger and thirst although I had no desire for any sustenance now other than my daughter's love.

Love. What a funny word for what our relationship was. I'd made mistakes, God knows I'd made mistakes, but there was always love. On my end, there was always love.

But, was it enough? Sadly, I didn't think so. Despite my best intentions, the poison in that house seeped into the next generation. Maybe Ellen's right. Maybe I should've tracked down the charming Denis, shamed him into doing the right thing by me. Make an honest woman of me. Honest, like a band of gold could do that after what I'd done.

Then Ellen would've had a daddy who loved her, who made her feel special. She would've had the white picket fence, happily-ever-after life that she's spent her life searching for. Instead, she was raised in that house, caught in the constant tug of war between myself and my mother. Always the pawn. No wonder. No wonder Ellen hates me.

But, the thought of some man's hands on me night after night. His sour breath on my face as he pounded away at me. A constant reminder of that bastard, that bastard who stole my innocence. A constant reminder of those times in the shed. No. I couldn't do it. I couldn't give up the safety of my spinster bed. Not for Ellen. Not for anyone.

And so now I had to pay the price of putting my own desires ahead of my daughter. If only a Hail Mary and an Our Father could atone for that sin.

It was late afternoon when I woke from my opium induced slumber. A late summer storm raged outside my window. The room was dark and without my glasses I could just make out that there was someone standing by the window. Her heels clicked on the tiles as she walked to me, her bright hair glowing in low light from the window. She handed me my glasses. "Hello, Mom."

"Ellen, you're back."

"I am." She stroked my hair. "And I'm not leaving again. I promise. I'm here to the end."

"To the end," I repeated faintly.

"Yes, Mom. To the end."

"Good," I replied. "Good."

Chapter 23

Ellen

"She's fading," I said into the phone. "She's fading fast. I know you're excited about getting ready for orientation, but if you want to say good bye, you need to come up in the next day or so."

"Timmy has to work tomorrow but he said he'd drive me up with me on Tuesday. I haven't spoken to Michael."

"I spoke to him. He's at the Cape with his roommate but he's taking the train down on Wednesday."

"Okay. Do you want me tell Dad?" Veronica asked hesitantly.

"Of course. Tell him you're coming up. But, there's no reason for him to miss work for this." I tried to keep the flint from my voice.

"But, it's Nana. Shouldn't he..."

"Leave it, Veronica. Just leave it. He had his chance to say good-bye." He had his chance.

"Are you sure? Because I could I ask him to come with me tonight and Timmy could drive down by himself."

"I'm sure, honey."

After I decided to put my doubts and anger aside and return to my mother's room, my mother was quiet but coherent. I spent the following handful of days reading the paper to her, reading the bible. She didn't seem to care what I read as long as I was with her, as long as she could hear my voice. But then yesterday something changed. She was agitated, her fingers constantly plucked at the bed covers for some reason. Short of knocking her out altogether, nothing seemed to calm her. Whenever she was awake she would look intently at the corner of her room, near the window. She nodded at it, murmured to it, as if she was speaking to someone. What upset me most of all was that she no longer recognized me. The forty-three year old Ellen, mother of three, was gone. In Rose's mind, that Ellen had been replaced by my grandmother.

The word had gone out and now members of the extended family streamed through the room. Auntie Maura, her sons, their wives and children, Paul's children, Carol's sister. Some sat naturally and chatted about an upcoming family wedding or graduation, as if my mother could follow what they were saying, as if she would be there for the happy event. Others were uncomfortable and spent more time talking to me rather than addressing my mother. One distant cousin was so rattled that she spent her half hour visit filling vases with water, even a vase full of artificial flowers.

Veronica and Timmy arrived around noon the next day. They walked into my mother's room bursting with youth and vitality, both their faces burnished with a thick layer of freckles. Timmy engulfed me in a suffocating hug. Veronica held back and offered me an uncertain smile.

Rose had just woken from a nap and was relatively alert. "Come here to me," she croaked to the children.

Veronica walked up to her and hesitantly took her hand. Timmy followed.

"Hello, Nana."

"Ellen, what have you done to your hair?"

"I'm not Ellen, I'm..."

"What has happened to your beautiful blonde hair?" She looked at me. "Mama, did you let Ellen dye her hair? Was it you or was it that devil Laurie Nolan?"

"But, Nana, I'm..."

"Red? Why on earth would you dye that poor child's hair red. I don't like it. I don't like it at all."

I shot Veronica a look. "It'll wash out, Rosie. The girls were only experimenting."

"Well, I should hope so," she huffed. During my own adolescence, Rose wouldn't have said a word if I had shaved my head. This new querulous personality of hers was strange and unsettling.

"And who is this, Ellie? Is it your boyfriend?"

Playing along, Timmy said, "Yes, I'm a friend from school." He contorted his face into an approximation of a smile, but I could see how upset he was. I sometimes forgot how young my children were, how sheltered. Their lives had been a whirl of private schools, sports, parties. Other than Brendan's remote parenting style, this

136

death was probably the first bit of sadness to touch their unblemished lives. But, Timmy was brave. He filled the space with stories from his summer life guarding job. Rose nodded, almost pleasantly, as if she could follow his stories.

It was Veronica I worried about. She shrank into the corner and stared blankly at her grandmother. I sensed that neither my mother nor my daughter could take much more, so I said, "Rose, it's time for you to rest. You can see the children later."

"Mama, I don't need you to tell me what to do," Rose snapped. "I'm a grown woman, with a child of my own. You seem to like to forget that."

"Of course," I soothed, "of course."

Tears sprung from her eyes. "Why are you always going off without me? Why don't you ever let me come?"

Veronica's eyes were wild now with panic and Timmy looked like he was going to cry.

"We're not going far, Rose. I promise, we're not going far."

After I settled the children back at the house, I returned to St. Francis. Sister Elizabeth was in with her. My mother continued that disturbing plucking motion, but it didn't seem to phase Sister Elizabeth. She continued her soothing patter while my mother mindlessly pulled at her covers. I stood at the doorway, unable to enter.

"Hey."

I turned around. "Hey yourself."

"Here, I thought you could use this." He handed me a large coffee.

I carefully sipped the hot coffee. "Thanks, Billy."

"How is she?"

I gestured to the open door. "Not good, as you can see for yourself. She hasn't much longer, I'm afraid."

"And you?"

"I'm here. I'm still here. That's about all I can say for myself."

He took my free hand. "Let's go outside. I think you could use a break."

We walked hand-in-hand to the empty courtyard, the late afternoon sun still strong. We sat together on the hard bench in front of Our Lady's statue.

"You look wiped out."

"Really?" I self consciously ran my fingers through my overgrown hair.

He touched my cheek. "You still look beautiful to me. You just look tired. Tired and sad."

I smiled. "Tired and sad. I guess that about sums it up."

"What can I do, Ellen? What do you need?"

"God, it's been a long time since anyone has asked me that."

"I'm here for you. Whatever you need."

"Molly's not due here until seven. I don't know if my uncles are coming so I'd like to stick around. My son and daughter are back at the house and they're pretty shook up about all of this. I don't think I have any food in the house. Would you mind dropping them off a pizza or something."

"Of course." Billy sounded grateful to be able to do something for me. "But, uh, who should I say I am?"

"A neighbor? A friend?" I ran my hand through his hair. "We can explain our, uh, relationship after..."

"It's okay, Ellen. We can take it slow. You don't have to make any decisions now."

I tried to smile. "Billy, you have been amazing. I don't know how I could've gotten through these past few weeks without you. I don't want this, us, to end. I don't."

He kissed me gently. "Neither do I."

"I need time to sort this out and I don't want to get my children involved right now. You understand, don't you?"

"I understand. Don't worry about any of this. Concentrate on getting through the next few days."

"Thank you, Billy."

When I returned to my mother's room, she was asleep, her breath a jagged rattle. Sister Elizabeth sat by the window, in full view of the courtyard.

"How is she?" I hoped Sister Elizabeth had somehow missed mine and Billy's kiss.

"The same, poor thing. She sees them, so it won't be long now."

"Them?" I sat in the chair across from Sister Elizabeth.

"Them. The spirits. The angels."

"Aw surely, Sister, you're an intelligent woman. You can't believe that."

She looked at me a moment, her wrinkled face solemn yet kind. "I am serious. I've been around death long enough to know what happens."

"With all due respect, Sister, I'm not sure I believe you."

"With all due respect, Ellen," she said tartly, "I don't need you to believe me. God and His messengers don't need your acknowledgement in order to exist and do their work."

I took Sister Elizabeth's hand and I said in a more conciliatory tone, "Sister, you've been so good to my mother, so good to me these past few weeks. I don't want to argue with you. And if my mother believes she's being visited by angels or whoever, so long as she's happy I guess I'm fine with it."

Sister gave me a hard look. "I didn't say she was happy. I said that she hasn't long now. She's fighting it. She's fighting them."

"Fighting?"

"Yes, fighting to stay alive."

"No, Sister, I think you're wrong. My mother has accepted her death."

"You're right, of course. She knows she's going to die. But yet, she's still holding on."

"To what? Holding on to what?" I asked.

"To you. I think she's holding on to her unfinished business with you."

"We have no more unfinished business, Sister. I told her I'd be with her to the end. She seemed happy with that."

"But have you told her that you love her?" Sister Elizabeth asked gently. "That you forgive her?"

"Our family's never been one for expressing our feelings. She knows that I'm here."

"Look, Ellen, I can't look into her head any better than I can look into yours but I believe that if you tell your mother these things, it will release her."

There was a moan from the bed as my mother continued to sleep fitfully.

"And end her suffering." I looked at my mother.

"Yes, end her suffering." Sister Elizabeth squeezed my hand. "And yours."

Sister Elizabeth walked over to my mother, whispered a prayer and then bent to kiss my mother on the forehead. Without another word, she left the room.

I sat alone with my mother. The weak afternoon sun barely penetrated through the room's small window. I walked to my mother and sat on her bed. I laid my hands on her poor battered body, shrunken and punctured with the tubes that brought her relief.

For some reason, I thought of the only time I could remember her smacking me. It was summertime. Me, the Conroy boys and the Griffins from down the street were playing hide and seek. I think I was around eight, maybe nine at the most. Billy Conroy, who I considered a baby at age six, kept following me wherever I hid. The two of us were huddled behind a bag of mulch in the shed. I poked Billy hard in the stomach because he kept sneezing.

"Stop sneezing," I whispered.

"Ow, stop hitting me. I can't help it."

"You're such a baby. Why don't you find your own hiding spot?"

The shed door flew open. I threw an old burlap bag over us. I was sick of being it. Someone lifted the bag. It was my mother. She roughly grabbed my arm and dragged me from the shed. She didn't seem to notice Billy.

"How many times? How many times have I told you not to go in that shed?"

My eyes squinted in the bright sun. "But, Mom, we were only..."

I looked up and her arm was lifted up in the air. With an almighty whack, she struck me across the backside. I could feel the sting through my thin terrycloth shorts. My eyes teared, not from the pain, because it didn't really hurt that much, but from the shock. My Granny gave me a smack every now and then, but never my mother. Never Rose.

She collapsed onto the lawn, her head in her hands. "Stay away from the shed. Never go in the shed."

Billy peeked out the door of the shed and when he saw Rose wasn't looking, he climbed the fence to his own front yard. My own eyes now dry, I stared at my mother.

She rocked back and forth. My quiet self contained mother who never cried, never yelled. Never spoke in anything but a calm clear voice. She moaned like a wounded animal.

I touched her shoulder and she flinched and gave a little shout that brought my grandmother to the front door.

"For goodness sake, what's going on?" Kitty climbed down the stairs and looked around to make sure none of the neighbors could see her hair in curlers. "Jesus, Rose, get hold of yourself." She looked at me. "What happened?"

"Nothing. I was playing in the shed and then Mom started yelling at me."

Kitty's face fell, her well rouged cheeks almost collapsed into themselves. "Get now, Ellie. Go play with your friends. I'll take care of your mother. She just had a bad turn. Too much sun."

I hesitated for a moment, but then walked down the stone steps to the children gathered in front of the Griffins' house. I could hear Granny say to my mother, "It's all right, Rosie. He's gone now. He's gone."

I looked down at my unconscious mother. What had those two put her through? What had I put her through? I stroked her hair. "Mom, it's Ellen," I said somewhat self-consciously. "I'm not sure if you can hear me or understand me, but I want you to know that I'm here. I'm here with you."

Her features remained still and didn't indicate whether she could hear me or not. Undeterred, I continued, "Mom, I know that things weren't easy for you. I don't know exactly what happened in that house, between you and Kitty and Peter. I do know that they hurt you, and for that I'm very sorry. I wish I'd known about all of this when I was growing up. I'd like to think that I would've been kinder to you. At least I hope I would've been."

My mother moved slightly in the bed.

"I'm sorry, Mom. I'm sorry for being so hard on you. I don't even know myself exactly why I acted that way. It was as if I couldn't help myself. I just wanted to badly to fit in, be like the other girls in their perfect houses, their perfect families. It's stupid, I know, and I'm too old to use that excuse. I forgive you, Mom, for not being who I wanted you to be. I hope you can forgive me for failing you as a daughter. Please forgive me, Mom."

Tears streamed down my face as I moved closer to her. I whispered in her ear, "I love you Mom. I love you and I forgive you. Now please, please go find your peace."

I was crying and holding her hand when Molly and Auntie Maura entered the room about a half hour later. They said nothing to me as they surrounded the bed.

Chapter 24

Rose

"Rose."

I looked to the corner of the room, the corner that had been glowing for the past few days. People would call to me from that corner, but I would turn my head, close my ears. I wasn't ready to talk to any of them. And I wasn't ready now.

"Rose, love, can you hear me?"

Despite myself, I looked into the corner. There stood my Auntie Margaret, her hair a black curtain against the golden light. Her eyes, while a watery blue in life, were now a bright, brilliant aquamarine. They were mesmerizing.

"I can," I said as petulantly as a spoiled child, "but I'm not ready to listen to you. I'm not ready to listen to any of you."

"Then listen to her, Rosie. Listen to Ellen."

As if I was underwater, I could hear the faint sounds of my daughter's voice. "...I'm sorry I was so hard on you... forgive me..."

"It's okay now, Rosie. You can come to me."

"No," I said to my aunt. I felt so alone, so hollow. Ellen's words washed over me. The words of a guilty and stressed woman. A duty bound woman. Ah, yes, my daughter had done her duty by me. No one, not even I, could fault her for that.

I thought about my life and wondered why the two most important people in it, my mother and my daughter, found it so hard to love me. To protect me. To accept me for who I was. What was so wrong with me that despite my best efforts they couldn't love me?

"I love you... I forgive you."

I looked at Auntie Margaret. "Does she really mean it, do you think? She's not just saying that, is she?"

"She really means it, Rosie. She loves you. She's always loved you. She allowed other concerns to block that, but in her heart, deep down, she always loved you."

I felt Ellen's soft hand on my own bony one. It was warm, hot almost, as if her love for me burned through it.

"She loves me."

"Yes, Rosie, she does. They all love you. All the people you touched here on earth."

"I was loved?"

"Of course, Rosie. You've always been loved." The light behind Auntie Margaret began to burn even brighter. "Rosie, there are others who want to tell you how much they love you. Your mother. Your father."

I looked at her, entranced by the colors in the light. Gold, purple, red.

Auntie Margaret stepped forward and reached for my hand. "We have the most beautiful flowers here, Rosie. So beautiful."

I felt light and for the first time in weeks, the dull throbbing in my head was gone. I took her hand.

* * *

Ellen

My mother's breath quickened. She gasped, open mouthed, as if she were one of Paul's fishes, fighting for its life. Maura and Molly laid their hands on her bedcovers and prayed while I stared at my mother transfixed.

"Go, Mom," I whispered. "Go."

She lifted her hand from the bed, fingers outreached as if grabbing for something. Or someone.

She gave one more rattling gasp and then her hand fell back to the bed.

"Molly!" Auntie Maura shouted. "Quick, open the window. So that her spirit can get out."

Molly struggled to open the small window. I ran over to help her and together we lifted the reluctant window wide open, wide enough for my poor mother's tortured soul to escape us.

Chapter 25

Ellen

My mother was laid out in the navy blue dress she wore to Molly's son's wedding last year. With her hair pulled back in a chic knot and her lips painted an uncharacteristic crimson, she looked more like an executive secretary than my meek mother. Her chin jutted out, stubbornly, not unlike my own. Funny how I never noticed this similarity when she was alive.

The afternoon viewing was well attended by the parishioners of St. Ann's and our various neighbors. I was surprised that my mother had had so many friends and admirers. There was even a young Hispanic day worker who came to pay his respects. He proudly handed me a bouquet of flowers and told me how my mother had treated him with respect when he was out of work and homeless. He assured me that things were better for him now, but that he never forgot Rose's kindness.

The evening viewing was for family and close friends only. My children were there of course; my son Michael still upset that he hadn't seen my mother before she passed. Veronica chatted with Sarah, Molly's daughter. Timmy was surrounded by Paul's two sons, one of whom would be joining him at Duke in the Fall. I circulated among the various relatives. My nose twitched from the overwhelming flower arrangements.

If it wasn't for the body in the corner, it was almost as if we were at the cocktail portion of a family wedding. Catching up with my various cousins, many of whom I hadn't seen in years, was nice. If it had been someone else's mother in the box I think I would've really enjoyed myself.

Barbara Conroy, elegant in a black suit, grabbed my hand as I passed. "I'm so sorry, Ellen. Rose was such a good woman, such a good neighbor."

"Thank you." I felt a little uncomfortable around Mrs. Conroy, unsure of how much she knew about my relationship with her son.

She seemed very caught up in her own social whirl, so perhaps she hadn't noticed how much time Billy had spent on Rose Hill these past few weeks.

She interrupted my thoughts. "Billy's parking the car." She gave me a tight smile. "He'll be in in a minute." I nodded. Barbara was no fool. She had noticed.

Lisa dragged me over to the corner and droned on about a list of the readings for the funeral mass she had worked on with Sister Elizabeth. Billy came in, looking very handsome in a surprisingly well-cut black suit. He smiled at me and rolled his eyes when he saw me cornered by Lisa; his eagle eyed mother didn't miss our exchange.

My sister-in-law Carol saved me from Lisa and introduced me to her mother who I hadn't seen since Carol and Danny's wedding. The mother, who was a bit deaf, was shouting in my ear when Brendan walked in.

"Sweetheart," he said in his booming voice. He confidently strode over to me and almost knocked over Carol's poor mother as he swept me into his arms.

"Brendan." I extricated myself from his embrace. "I didn't expect to see you here."

"Ah, boss, I know I'm a little late, but my insider trading case settled today." He looked around, as if he expected a round of applause. "I came here as soon as I could."

"I'm sure you did," I said lightly, not wanting to make a scene in front of the relatives.

"How are you?" Brendan asked.

"As well as could be expected."

"You look great!" He tapped the woman standing near him on the shoulder. "Doesn't she look great?"

My old friend Laurie Nolan, one of the few people I had confided in about Billy, spun around. She smiled hesitantly at me.

"Doesn't she?" Brendan continued to ask. "Miss, um, I'm sorry but have we met."

She extended her hand. "Laurie Nolan."

"Yes, Laurie Nolan," I said. "The maid of honor at our wedding. Ring any bells?"

"Oh, Laurie, of course," Brendan said, trying to recover. "I think you changed your hair."

"Brendan, why don't you walk over with me and pay your respects to my mother."

"Of course, sweetheart, of course. Nice seeing you again Laura."

Laurie rolled her eyes.

As we walked over to the casket, Brendan noticed Billy talking to Timmy and Veronica and his affable countenance quickly evaporated. "What is he doing here?" Brendan spat. "Why is he talking to our children?"

"The Conroys have been our neighbors for years," I said in a low voice. "Don't make a scene."

We knelt in front of the body. With his head bowed, he said, "I want him gone. Now."

"Shush, have some respect for my mother. Please."

Brendan quickly mouthed a Hail Mary, carelessly crossed himself and then stormed off to the men's room. As I made my way over to my Auntie Maura, Barbara Conroy stopped me. "Ellen, dear, I'm not feeling well. Billy and I are going to leave, but we'll see you at St. Ann's tomorrow. All right?"

Barbara didn't look at all sick, but I appreciated her tact. I nodded and accepted her embrace. Looking over her shoulder, Billy smiled at me. Brendan's little scene by the casket didn't exactly go unnoticed.

The rest of the wake went pretty much as I'd expected. Sister Elizabeth led a round of the rosary, the younger people stumbled through it. There was a lot of hugging, a lot of "isn't it a shame we only meet at funerals?" A lot of promising to do a better job of staying in touch. Despite how far the descendants of the O'Connor sisters had spread across both state and socio-economic lines, there was something almost primal in our need to be together to mark the passing of another member.

Brendan of course walked around the room as if he was the mayor. Making jokes with this one, slapping the back of another. I overheard him telling Paul how wonderful Duke is, how much it's made a man of our Timmy. As if he'd know. As if he'd ever even step foot on the campus.

Brendan had taken a cab from the airport so the five of us piled into my car—one big happy family. Of course Brendan along with my children were staying at my mother's house. Well, I guess technically it's my house now. After living alone in the house for so many weeks it felt strange to have them there. Brendan with his booming voice and my boys with their six foot frames overwhelmed the small house.

"Hey, boss, I'm starving. What do you have to eat around this place?"

"I don't think I have much. There might be some snacks in the boathouse."

"Let's order a pizza. Kids, do you want some Lawn Guyland pizza?"

"Sure!" Timmy said enthusiastically, always eager to be Brendan's side kick.

Veronica, who sat in the corner of the small kitchen table said, "Dad, do you really think it's appropriate to throw a pizza party when Nana just died. What about Mom?"

"Aw, come on sweetheart. A guy's gotta eat!"

I was surprised by Veronica. Like the boys, she loved to bask in Brendan's attention, no matter how fleeting. It was not like her to criticize him, to not serve as his permanent cheerleader. Perhaps these past few weeks sharing the house with him alone had given her some insight into her father. Not that I was happy to see it. I preferred that my children live in the happy family bubble I worked so hard to construct. However, given that I suspected I would soon be sticking a pin in that bubble, maybe her new awareness was not the worst thing in the world. "Veronica, it's all right. I don't mind. Let the boys have their pizza."

Thirty minutes later, Brendan and the boys drank the beers Michael found in the boathouse and inhaled pepperoni pizza. Veronica and I sipped ice tea and I was able to eat half a slice.

"Isn't it great to be here all together," Brendan said between enormous bites of pizza. "When we get back, I want to make this a regular thing. How about every Friday being pizza night?"

"Dad, I'm leaving for school next week." Veronica barely looked up from her plate.

"Yeah, me too," said Michael. "But, I'd definitely be up for it when we're back from break."

"Terrific! It'll be a new Mills family tradition. Every Friday. Sound good, honey?"

Veronica eyed me skeptically. I said noncommittally, "We'll see what everyone's schedules look like in the fall. Now Veronica, could you get those sheets out of the dryer? I want to make up the beds."

Veronica would be sleeping in my mother's room, Timmy in my room and Michael in Paul's old bed. The only place for me and Brendan to sleep was in the master bedroom, Kitty's old room. While I didn't look forward to sharing a bed again with Brendan, especially after what happened last time, I wanted things to appear as normal as possible for the children's sake. I needed to get through the funeral with as little drama as possible. I'd deal with my marriage and my affair after that.

I was already in bed, dressed in a very unsexy white cotton nightgown, when Brendan came in. He flipped the light on and then slowly undressed.

"It was great seeing everyone tonight, wasn't it? We should invite them down to the house soon. You could have a little, oh I don't know, a little family reunion. Wouldn't that be great?"

"I don't know, Brendan. You've never been interested in entertaining my family before."

"There a great group of folks, and you know it's a time like this that you realize what's really important. Family. That's what it's all about."

"That's what it's all about, huh?"

"Absolutely." Brendan jumped into the bed, naked.

"Aren't you forgetting something?"

"What?" Brendan asked, feigning innocence.

"Your pajamas. Aren't you forgetting your pajamas?" This time I didn't even try and hide my irritation.

"Ooops, must've forgotten to pack them."

"Brendan, who do you think you're talking to? Those ridiculous pajamas are always the first thing you pack."

"Well, my lovely bride will just have to warm me up." Brendan snuggled closer to me.

"I'm tired and I don't have the patience for this."

"Sweetheart, I know that you've been under a lot of pressure, stress, these past few weeks. Once we get home everything will be better."

"Better?"

"With us. Things will be better with us. I realized how much you mean to me. I want to do whatever it takes to get us back on track."

"Back on track? Brendan, please be real. We haven't been on any sort of track for years."

"Well, it's never too late, right? We could try that, what's it called? Marriage counseling. We could try that marriage counseling you suggested."

"You mean the marriage counseling I suggested ten years ago? That marriage counseling?"

"Yeah, sure. Let's do that."

"And what's prompted this renewed interest in our relationship? Did Christine break up with your or is it the fact that I'm fucking someone else?"

"Honestly, is it a crime to have a new appreciation for my beautiful wife?"

"I can't deal with this bullshit now. I really can't. I've been begging you for your love, hell even just your attention, for years now. All of sudden you care about me, about the kids? Now you want to have a pizza night? It's pathetic. A day late and a dollar short." I turned over, my back to him. "I have to bury my mother tomorrow. I need to get through the next twenty-four hours without having a complete breakdown. The last thing I need to think about right now is this marriage so can you please act like a normal person and go through the motions tomorrow? If you really do love me, then do that. Show me that for once in your life you can think of someone other than yourself."

"Okay, Ellen. I can do that." He patted my shoulder gently. "You go to sleep now."

The next morning, the five of us got ready in silence. The Griffins from down the street had left us a plate of bagels, rolls and cream cheese. Timmy made a pot of coffee and we ate breakfast. My hand shook a little when I was trying to put on my mascara, but other than that, I held it together fairly well.

We gathered at the funeral home one more time. Sister Elizabeth, dressed in a simple black dress, led us in a prayer. Each of my uncles walked up to the coffin; Danny bravely grabbed her hand, Paul slipped a miniature sailboat into the casket. Each of my children quickly said goodbye to her. And then it was my turn.

I knelt before what remained of my mother and bowed my head. Silently, I begged for her forgiveness. I prayed that she had finally found peace. I stepped back to allow them to close the casket. As the lid fell across her face, my knees buckled. Molly was behind me. She roughly grabbed my elbow and broke my fall.

"You're doing wonderfully, Ellen. Just a few more hours, and you'll be done. Okay?"

"I'm okay. I just..."

"I know."

Molly and I followed my uncles out into the limo. Brendan drove the children in my car. Auntie Maura rode with us while her sons followed behind. We slowly proceeded to St. Ann's. The sun was blazing when we reach the church. My silk blouse clung to me, already damp from the heat. Dizzy as I climbed out of the limo, the sun blinded me. I stumbled slightly. A strong hand grabbed me. Billy.

I turned to him, his golden hair brilliant in the sun. I leaned on him as he wordlessly guided me up the stone steps into the church. The vestibule was dark, cool. I stopped for a moment.

"Are you all right, Ellen? Do you want a drink of water?"

"Yes. I could use some water."

Billy got me a cup from the hall bathroom. I drank the lukewarm water, and felt marginally better. Billy then walked me to the front of the church and held my arm as if he was afraid that I would fall. Like a father walking a bride down the aisle, Billy deposited me at the altar. He squeezed my hand as he left to find his way to a pew in the middle of the church, behind those reserved for close friends and family. I walked over to the organist, a small wizened man of at least seventy. I'd promised my mother before she died that I would sing a song at her funeral mass. It seemed like an easy enough request at the time; I'd always liked to sing. But now, my lungs felt like they were made of lead and the last thing I wanted to do was face a room full of people.

But I was not about to fail my mother again, so I stood at the lower lectern, my shoulders straight. People streamed into the church, and once again I was surprised by the size of the crowd, especially for a weekend in mid-August, the height of vacation time. My mother, who I'd always thought of as a semi-recluse, had clearly touched a lot of people in this town.

151

When the priest gave us the signal, the organist began his dirge. I opened my mouth, but nothing came out. Not missing a beat, the organist continued to play, as if this was just part if the introduction. I looked out at my daughter. She nodded her head at me, encouraged me. I tried again, and sang out:

"Be not afraid, for I am with you always,

Come, follow me, and I will give you rest."

The mass was beautiful, every reading and song picked with care by my mother and Sister Elizabeth. By the end of the priest's eulogy, I didn't think I had any more tears left, but then he invited Sister Elizabeth to say a few words and by the end of that I don't believe there was a dry eye in the church. Veronica sat next to me, her arm around me. Brendan sat on my other side where he awkwardly patted my arm from time to time.

My two sons were pallbearers along with my uncles. I followed them down the aisle with Veronica on my right and Brendan on my left. Billy boldly stared at us as we walked down the aisle, his mouth tight.

Brendan insisted on riding in the limo to St. Charles cemetery, as if to stake his claim to me. I was too worn out to protest. I refused to meet Billy's eyes as he stood on the church steps next to his mother.

The twenty minute ride to St. Charles was a blur. The air conditioning was spotty in the back of the limo and my brow was slick with sweat. Once we reached the cemetery there was hardly any relief. Located smack dab in the middle of the Island, there was no sea breeze to ameliorate the sweltering August heat. Molly looked wilted. Only Brendan, a native Washingtonian, seemed unfazed by the heat and humidity. He took my hand and it was all I could do not to snatch it back. But, my children were there, as was my extended family. Now was not the time to publicly show the deep fissures of my marriage.

My grandmother's grave was open, ready to receive her daughter. No one commented how odd it was that despite having two husbands, Kitty chose to share her grave only with her daughter. The cars lined up as the flushed Irish faces gathered around the gravesite. The funeral home's worker bees wordlessly handed each of us a flower: a daisy, a lily, a blood red rose.

152

Monsignor Ryan lead us in yet another Hail Mary. An Our Father. A Glory Be. Sweat streamed down my back and all I could think, God help me, was how badly I wanted this to be over. I had no more prayers left in me, and what had initially given me comfort, now only left me numb.

Monsignor Ryan invited me, as Rose's only child, to place my flower on her casket. The casket was raised above the open grave on a pulley. I threw my rose onto the casket, but I must have thrown it too hard because it slid off and fell down into the open grave. Down onto my Granny's casket.

Veronica followed, her lily landed on top of my mother's casket. The twins added their blossoms, and then my uncles, their wives. Soon the casket was covered with flowers, the smell of them, overripe in the heat, slightly dizzying.

Paul invited everyone to the obligatory lunch at an Italian restaurant one mile from St. Charles. Once again, Brendan staked his claim on me by placing his large palm on my sweaty back as we walked to my car. I didn't know why he bothered, really. Billy and Barbara Conroy hadn't followed us to the gravesite. But my children, despite the circumstances, seemed to find comfort in the fact that their parents were in the same place for once and I didn't want to cause any more dissent, so while I didn't overtly acknowledge his touch, I didn't shy away from it either.

Most of the crowd at the gravesite were close relatives, about forty or so, and the trail of cars crawled in the summer traffic to Giamellis Restaurante. The restaurant had arrange the table in a large horseshoe. I sat on the left, next to Auntie Maura. Brendan sat next to me and Lisa was on his right. I looked with disinterest at the prix fix menu that Paul had selected as I sipped the house white wine, so parched I barely registered its metallic aftertaste.

The room hummed as the Irish relatives feasted on antipasto. Auntie Maura, despite herself, was enjoying her time among the family and away from the persistently cheery pastel walls of the Sunny Hills Assisted Living Centre. Her easy patter with Carol's mother, another widow, was soothing and didn't require me to do much more than nod occasionally. On the other hand Brendan's voice boomed across the room. My two sons sat enthralled as their father recounted how he swayed the jury in his clearly guilty client's favor. Having heard many iterations of this story over the years, I was able to smile, somewhat vacantly, and say "uh-huh" and "really" in all the right places without straining my brain too much.

I had my mouth full seafood ravioli when I overheard Brendan said, "Sure. Just send us over the paperwork and we can get it taken care of."

I turned to him. "What paperwork?"

"For the sale."

"Sale?"

As if talking to an invalid, Brendan said slowly, "The sale of your mother's house."

"What are you talking about?"

Lisa piped in. "Ellen, dear, we had three realtors in to appraise the house. We're offering you a very fair price, especially given the house's condition."

"Don't you worry about a thing, sweetheart," Brendan soothed. "I'll take care of everything."

I felt a humming in my head. With effort, I said slowly, "I'm not selling the house."

Brendan rubbed my arm. "But honey, what are you going to do with it?"

"I don't know, but it's my house and I'm not selling it."

"Ellen, be reasonable," Lisa said, her broad face still shiny with sweat. "You could barely take care of it when you were living in it. How will you take care of things from Washington?"

"I don't care. I'm not selling it to you. I'm not selling it to anyone."

"But, we spent over forty thousand dollars on the boat house! We always assumed that Rose would leave the house to Paul and Danny, or at least split it three ways between the three of you. No one expected her to leave it only to you. It's not fair."

"My mother paid a high price for that house." I looked at Molly. Molly nodded.

"But, it's not fair," Lisa said, looking to Paul for support.

"It was my father's house. And my grandfather's. By rights it should belong to me and Danny," Paul said with an uncharacteristic cold fury. "I shouldn't have to pay for my own house, but I'm trying to be fair. I'm trying to do the right thing here and you're being completely unreasonable."

"Too bad, Paul. It's my house now. Rosie's bastard owns your father's house. I hope he's spinning in his grave." The room was quiet now, all eyes on me.

Paul slammed down his glass. Red wine splattered across the table. "Jesus Christ, Ellen. We've all put up with enough of your shit. You waltz in here, play the martyr card. 'Oh feel sorry for me, my mother's dying.' The mother you ignored for years. The tears, the scenes. Meanwhile you're off fucking the neighbor."

Auntie Maura gasped.

"Oh, don't deny it," Paul continued. "We all know. Everyone on Rose Hill knows."

Danny took hold of Paul's arm. "That's enough, Paul. Not in front of the children."

"Nice, Paul, nice. I may not have been a perfect daughter, but I'm nothing compared to you and that fat bitch. My mother's not even cold and you vultures are already circling in for the kill!"

Lisa's face was bright red. "How dare..."

"Shut up, Lisa. Just shut up. And you," I said looking at Brendan. "Get the car and take me home. To my house."

Veronica's eyes were the size of saucers, but I didn't have the energy to comfort her. I didn't have the energy for any of them. Molly told me that she'd make sure the kids got home. I think I nodded at her.

Brendan brought the car around the front and for the first ten minutes in the car he was smart and shut his mouth. But Brendan's a compulsive talker and so he eventually said, "And you complain about my family."

"Brendan..."

"Ellen, what got into you back there? You know you have to sell that house."

"Why?"

"What do you mean why? Because we live in Washington. Because there's no reason to keep the house."

I stared at the traffic on Route 110. The relentless summer sun beat down on the minivans, the mini-malls, a giant big-box outlet store. The road hummed with the banalities of suburban life and I found it somewhat comforting. What I wouldn't do right now to just pull into the store and distract myself with discount toilet paper and garbage bags. While stopped at a red light, I stared at a young mother struggling with a toddler and a bulky ten set roll of paper towels. "It's mine. I don't need a reason to keep it."

"Jesus, Ellen, have you completely lost your mind? You've always hated that house. It's old. It's small."

Without looking at him, I said, "I don't care."

Brendan then adopted a reasonable, resonant tone. One I'm sure he'd used at many settlement meeting to great effect. Its low tone implicitly said trust me, I'll take care of you. I'm sure many of his opponents fell for it. Hell, I'd fallen for it for over twenty years. "Look, honey, Lisa and Paul are offering a very fair price. And he's got a point. It was his family's house. I know that you have some kind of bug up your ass about it, but that's the grief talking. You haven't been yourself these past few weeks. You're doing things, that I know you wouldn't normally do. That you must regret."

I turned to face him. "Are you referring to Billy? Because for your information, I don't regretted one delicious minute that we've spent together."

"Ellen, please. Do you really think this fling will survive the weekend? You could never be happy with a nobody like him. Can you imagine taking him to the club? Or to Parent's Weekend at Duke?"

"Parents' Weekend at Duke? As if you'd know anything about Parents' Weekend at Duke."

He patted my leg reassuringly. "We'll pack you up and get you home and use the money from Paul to buy a weekend home. You always said that you wanted to buy something on the Delaware shore."

"Yeah, and you always said you didn't have the time."

"Well, now I'll make the time. Come on, sweetie, let's just go home and put this all behind us."

"Go home to what."

"To our life. Our life together."

"What life together?"

"Oh, Jesus, not this again. Let's just go home and we'll sort it out there. I've got an early morning meeting anyway, so we'll just pack up and leave tonight."

"I can't go home tonight. You know we have the *toradh do bhean muirneach*."

"The what?"

156

"It's an O'Connor family tradition. All the women have cake for the deceased."

"Haven't you spent enough time with these people?"

"These people? I thought you said they were fine people. That you couldn't wait to spend more time with them? Didn't you offer to host the next family reunion at our house."

Brendan blew through a red light. A minivan leaned heavily on its horn. "Shit, Ellen, I say a lot of things."

"That you do, Brendan. That you do."

We were silent then, and I closed my eyes and rested until we pulled up the driveway.

"Jesus, Ellen. Who's that?"

I opened my eyes and saw Denis sitting uncomfortably on the front porch.

"It's my brother."

Brendan threw the car into park. "What do you mean, brother?"

"I found my father last month. He had three other children."

"But, what..."

I didn't stop to listen to whatever Brendan had to say. I got out of the car and called out, "Hello, Denis."

Denis stood up awkwardly. "Hello, sister."

I slammed the car door. "So you know? How?"

"It didn't take a detective. You look just like my sister Anne Marie. And you left this on the kitchen table." Denis handed me the photocopy of the photo that had caused so much upheaval these past few weeks.

Brendan walked over to me and holding out his hand to Denis, said hello.

"Denis, this is my husband. He's just packing. Why don't we go down to the boathouse to talk?"

"Oh, I'm sorry. Have I come at a bad time? Is it your mother?"

"We just came back from the funeral."

"Oh, geez. Great timing, huh? Why don't I come back another time?"

"No, it's fine. In fact, I could use the distraction." I took Denis by the arm and turned without saying anything further to Brendan. As we walked across the road, Brendan slammed my mother's front door.

I settled Denis on a deckchair while I rummaged through the boathouse kitchen. I managed to find two cold beers and a bag of peanuts.

"Sorry, this is the best I could do."

"No, this is perfect." Denis took the beer from me. "What a view. This is a beautiful spot. It must have been great growing up here."

"It was, in a way."

"My Dad loves the water. He'd love this view. He spends as much time as he can at Jones Beach. When we were growing up, he'd pack a big cooler and load up the car and we'd spend hours on the beach. He used to get so mad at my mother, who was Italian, because she'd throw on a little oil and tan after one weekend. Poor Dad, he'd burn, peel, freckle, burn again. But it was fun. Of course he'd be half in the bag by noon and passed out by three, but it was still fun."

"It sounds like it."

"Yeah, well, no one's family is perfect, right?"

"I just screamed at my aunt who's trying to steal this house in front of an entire restaurant, so I agree with you there. No family's perfect."

"God, funerals. You should have seen my mother's. What a circus. In fact, I think that's a big part of why my father treated you the way he did. My sister went completely ballistic at the funeral. Told my father he wasn't welcome in her house, you know, the whole nine yards. I'll admit the old man was drunk, but hell, when was he not? And he adored my mother. Maybe he wasn't the best husband in the world, but he loved her and she loved him. And he's been lost without her."

"I'm sorry," I said, not knowing what else to say.

"Well, don't be sorry. It accomplished one good thing, I guess. He got sober and he made up with my sister. But, to tell you the truth, I think he was better off as a drunk. He drank for so long it was part of his personality. And God, was he funny. But now, it's like he doesn't know who he is. He doesn't know who to be without the booze."

We sat for a while in companionable silence. I went and got us two more beers.

"I hope you don't mind, but I told my brother Dominic about you. He'd like to meet you. He lives in Glen Cove with his wife and three kids, so it's not too far from here. He's always been hard on my father, maybe too hard, but Dom's a good guy. A good brother."

"I'd like that," I said simply.

"We haven't told Anne Marie. I don't think she's ready. I don't know when she'll be ready, to tell you the truth."

"I don't want to cause any trouble for your family. For your father."

"I'd like to get to know you. Now that I know you exist, I can't ignore the fact that you're out there. It ain't right. I told my old man that."

"So he knows you're here?"

"He knows. And I think he's glad that I'm here."

"Well, I'm glad too."

We chatted for a while about Denis' job, his recent divorce. We were just getting ready to walk back to the main house when Billy's boat docked. Billy, once again shirtless, easily jumped from the boat carrying his fishing gear. I waved him over.

"There's someone I'd like you to meet, Denis."

Billy ambled over. We had spent many hours discussing my father so Billy wasn't surprised to see Denis. The two men gave each other hearty handshakes while I looked on. The three of us were drinking the last three beers left in the boathouse when Brendan stomped onto the deck.

"Well, isn't this cozy?"

"Hello," I said, barely looking up. Nominally polite, but not inviting.

"I've spoken to our children. They're at Molly's in case you're interested. I'm flying back to D.C. with the boys tonight. Molly said she'd bring Veronica back here for that cake thing. I assume she can sleep here tonight?"

"Of course she can sleep here tonight."

"I didn't know if you'd be busy," he sneered.

"When have I been too busy to care for my daughter? That's your bailiwick, Brendan, not mine."

Brendan ignored my dig. "When can I expect you home?"

Billy wouldn't meet my eyes and Denis seemed slightly uncomfortable so I just said lightly, "I'll be in touch."

"Fantastic. I'll call myself a cab since you're busy." Brendan's face was uncharacteristically flushed with anger. He glared at me for a moment and then spun around and left.

Billy finished his beer in a final gulp. "I'd better get going. My mother's waiting for this fish. I'll call you later, El."

"Okay. I'll be here."

He smiled, did the nice to meet yous with Denis and then walked to his mother's.

After Billy left, Denis smiled. "Was it my imagination or are things a little complicated around here?"

I laughed. "You're some detective. Things are a lot complicated around here. I suspect that I'll have to make a lot of decisions in the next few weeks. I didn't just bury my mother, I feel like I've buried a lot of my past, especially with respect to my marriage. But I've uncovered some things as well. I don't think I ever really appreciated how much not knowing about my father affected me. I think it was one of the things that poisoned my relationship with my mother. I can see now how it impacted the choices I made later on, who I chose to marry. And while I'm disappointed that he doesn't want me in his life, at least I've met him. I know where he is. I feel at peace in a way."

"You're a nice woman, Ellen. I hope that things work out for you. I hope my father changes his mind and that you get to meet my brother and sister. And I hope whether you move to D.C. or wherever, that we can stay in touch."

"I would love that, Denis. You have no idea how much."

Chapter 26

Ellen

Brendan barely looked at me as he walked out the door and into the waiting cab. A few months ago, I would have been thrilled that he showed so much attention to me, to our marriage. I didn't know if it was meeting Billy or losing my mother, but his feelings, his actions, they all now left me cold. If I never had to see him again, I'd be just as happy. How strange. I'd spent twenty years catering to him, tying myself up in knots to get his attention. Although I should've been sad about the death of my feelings for my husband, I wasn't sad. I felt calm. Free.

I stood underneath a punishing stream of hot water for twenty minutes, the rough porcelain of the old tub scratched the soles of my feet. I carefully climbed over the tub onto the old mat and stared at my red face in the mirror. I rubbed my mother's lilac body lotion into my skin and dressed in a blue linen shift. I walked into my mother's room and opened her small wooden jewelry box. Inside were her rosary beads and the silver St Brigid's cross my grandmother had bought Rose on her sole trip back home to Ireland. I slipped the delicate chain around my neck.

Downstairs, I rummaged through the cabinets and searched for the candles that were probably last used for Kitty's *toradh do bhean muirneach*. I arranged the candles around the living room and the adjoining dining room. I opened the small china breakfront and carefully removed the china plates, cups and saucers that were Kitty's pride and joy. I washed and dried them and then set the table. After my performance at the funeral lunch I wasn't sure who was going to show up for the *toradh do bhean muirneach*, but I wanted to be prepared.

It was almost dark when Carol arrived with her a plate of cannoli. Only female blood relations were supposed to attend a *toradh do bhean muirneach*, but Carol was so sweet and had been so good to my mother that I decided to make an exception. No such exception was made for Lisa. Given the now bad blood between me and my uncles I was touched that Carol decided to cross enemy lines.

Molly soon arrived with her daughter Sarah, my Veronica and of course Auntie Maura. Veronica smiled at me, in her funny, wry way. I wasn't sure what to expect from her. She liked to play the worldly miss, but really she's been a very sheltered little girl. I certainly would've liked to break the news of my relationship with Billy in a different way, but oddly she didn't seem too bothered by it. I hoped my sons would be as understanding.

Maura very proudly set out the soda bread she'd managed to make in her Sunny Hills efficiency kitchen. "Who brought cannoli to a *toradh do bhean muirneach*?"

"What? Was that wrong?" Carol asked.

I laughed. "That's what happens when you open up the party to Italians."

"I'll take my cannoli over that pound cake any day!"

Maura took the seat at the head of the table, as was her place as the oldest. "Soda bread, love, and it'll melt in your mouth, I promise you that."

Molly placed her apple cake next to the cannoli. "We've enough cake here to feed an army. Maybe we should've invited some of the men."

"Men!" Maura was horrified. "Men at a *toradh do bhean muirneach*. God forbid."

"Well, they can have the leftovers," Carol said.

"We burn the leftovers, love." Maura said. "For the spirits."

"Oh, the spirits," Carol said. "Of course."

Veronica and Sarah made tea, and I lit the candles. Molly had brought some pictures which she set up on the table. My mother in her holy communion dress, her straight black hair coaxed into ringlets; one of Rose holding me as an infant; Molly and my mother on a beach last year. Molly even surprised me by adding the picture of my mother in her postulant's veil.

The room was lit entirely by candlelight, everyone's face casted partially in shadow.

"Auntie Maura, what do we do now?" Veronica asked. "Do we chant or something?"

"Chanting? For goodness sake, child. What do you think this is, a séance?"

"Well, you did mention spirits."

"It's a custom, that's all. No, we eat cake and bid our dear Rose farewell in our own way. The old people used to think that the spirit needed sustenance to make its long journey to heaven. I don't know about that, but I would like to believe that Rose is here with us now."

"And I happen to know that she loved my cannoli," Carol added. Molly laughed.

"Does everyone in Ireland do this?" Sarah asked. Both she and Veronica were too young to be included in Kitty's *toradh do bhean muirneach* so this was their first one.

"I don't know, love. I know all the women in our family did it and I believe a few other families in Kilvarren did as well. I remember attending one of the Sheehan's, since they're our third cousins. I don't know about other parts of Ireland. Remember, I left there in the 1940s and I've only been back once. I've never even been to Dublin."

"What does that word mean? It sounds like you got some cake caught in your throat," Sarah giggled.

"How dare you mock our mother tongue, you pup. *Toradh do bhean muirneach*," Maura said slowly. "It means wake for a beloved woman, although we always do it after the funeral so I guess technically it's not a wake."

"And why are only women allowed to come?" Veronica asked.

"All these questions." Maura sipped her tea. "Ah, I don't know. To get the men out of our hair for a few hours?"

"I think it's a lovely custom." I poured everyone out their tea. "I wasn't sure I was up for this but now I'm glad you're all here."

Maura bit into the apple cake. "Molly, this is delicious."

"It's my mother's recipe."

"Margaret always did make nice cake," Maura said. "I'll have to be sure to give you the recipe for my soda bread, Molly. For my *toradh do bhean muirneach*. I know I can't rely on this one to make it."

"I can order it from a bakery." I smiled at her and played the fool.

"A bakery? Please, soda bread from a bakery? You might as well serve cannoli."

"I'll take the recipe, Maura," Molly said, "but I hope I don't have to make it for a *toradh do bhean muirneach* for a long, long time."

"Won't be long now, love. Now that those bitches have stuck me in that place. Sunny Hill. They might as well call it Death Hill. I swear, they're dropping like flies on my floor. There were two last week."

Molly rubbed Maura's shoulder. "Auntie, no. Don't say that."

"Death is part of life, girls. It comes for us all. Besides, I miss my sisters. I miss my husband. I want to see my baby daughter again. I know it sounds odd to you, but I'm looking forward to it."

Veronica and Sarah looked slightly horrified.

I smiled at the girls. "We'll just make the most of the time we have together." I poured Maura more tea. "That's a lesson I learned too late with my own mother. I wish I had gotten to know her better and didn't wait until she was on her deathbed."

Maura set down her tea cup. "Hush now, love. You were with her when it counted. A *toradh do bhean muirneach* is not for regrets. It's a time to celebrate. Tell us something good you remember about your mother. Something funny."

"Something funny?" I was stuck, I couldn't think of anything light, anything funny. My last few months with my mother were so heavy with dark emotions: anger, guilt, regret.

Molly seemed to have sensed my confusion. "Give us a song then, Ellen. You're the only one here who can carry a note and your mother loved to hear you sing."

"What should I sing?"

Veronica said, "Anything, Mom. What about that song you sang me as a baby?"

I stood up and sang the snippets of the songs my mother sang to me as a child, the songs I sang to my own children. Some in English, some in fractured Irish. I stumbled over some of the words, but Veronica, in her deep raspy voice, supplied the missing words. Maura clapped along, slightly off beat.

"Oh, that was wonderful, Ellen," Molly said when I was finished. "I'm sure Rosie loved that."

"Thanks, Molly. I hope she did."

"I can't think of anything funny," Molly said. "Rosie was never exactly the life of the party. But, she was always there for me.

Always listening, always helping. I loved her so much and I know that I'll miss her every day for the rest of my life."

"She was a dear, sweet girl who had to put up with a lot. But she never complained. Not once." Auntie Maura reached into her bag and pulled out a small bottle of whiskey. "Veronica, dear, go get me those glasses out of the cabinet. I want to toast Rosie and I need something a little stronger than tea."

Veronica pulled out the crystal glasses. Maura, her hand shaking, insisted on pouring the whiskey herself. Veronica handed us each a glass.

"*Slainte*, girls. To Rose."

"To Rose," we all repeated.

Epilogue

Two Years Later

"Stop fidgeting or I'll burn your neck."

"Geez, Laurie, you're taking forever."

"Stop, you want this to be perfect, don't you? You only get married once. Okay, twice in your case."

A cool breeze blew through the window. Outside, my future mother-in-law instructed the catering crew how to set up the tents on our two adjoining lawns. One benefit of being a divorced Catholic was that the second time around you didn't have to bother with the Church's rules. No ceremony in a dark church, no boring Pre Cana classes.

Billy had wanted to have a destination wedding in the Bahamas but I surprised him by insisting that we get married on Rose Hill. My first wedding was so rushed that most of my family didn't make it. I'd worn an off the rack shapeless sack with enough room around the middle to hide my baby bump. Now, twenty-odd years on, I was fit from my daily runs with Billy and I wanted to wear something slinky, sexy. I also wanted my family, all of my family, around me for this trip down the aisle.

"So you're not upset that you're not my matron of honor?" I asked Laurie as I sipped the champagne that Brendan, Christine and baby Julia had sent as a wedding present.

"No, not at all. I'm sure Veronica will bring you better luck than I did."

"I hope so." I looked around the bedroom that Billy had transformed into a bright, airy yet luxurious escape. Billy and his crew had gutted the entire house down to the studs and updated it with only the best the materials and appliances. He even installed one of those tricked out showers which we had made good use of. The grounds and the outside still reminded me of my childhood, of my mother and my grandmother, but the changes on the inside made it my home. Mine and Billy's.

166

Laurie finished my hair and began my makeup. Given that Billy and I practically lived on either his boat or his motorcycle, Laurie had to use both foundation and powder to cover my stubborn freckles.

"Perfect. Just perfect."

I turned around to look at myself in the full length mirror. My hair was swept up in a soft, almost Grecian up-do. Paired with a simple, yet elegant, raw silk gown with a plunging neckline, the look was just right for a second wedding.

"Oh, Mom. You look beautiful."

Veronica stood in the doorway and for once wasn't wearing her customary wry smile. She looked young and bright and happy. Yes, happy. An O'Connor woman happy? Well, four generations in, it was about time.

After the funeral, after I told the children that I was taking a job with the SEC's New York office and leaving their father, my boys rallied around me. They respected their father, they wanted his approval and his attention, but I was the one they loved, the one they adored. I didn't know what to expect from Veronica. Our relationship was more layered, more prickly. And she was always a daddy's girl, or at least always wanted to be a daddy's girl. So despite her accepting behavior at the toradh do bhean muirneach, her response still surprised me. Not one word of recrimination, not one sulky look or tantrum. She was wonderful, really. My downtown office was near NYU so we often met for lunch and her latest boyfriend lived in neighboring Smithtown so I saw her on weekends as well.

"Thank you, sweetheart. So do you."

"And I haven't even gotten my hands on her yet. Sit down here, Veronica, and let me work my magic."

"I don't want my hair too big." Veronica reluctantly took my place in front of Laurie's deadly curling iron.

"This is Long Island for heaven's sake. Big hair is practically a county ordinance!" Laurie shook her own very sleek bob.

I smiled. "Laurie, go easy on her."

"You two are no fun. Where's Carol when I need her?"

I looked out the window again. Carol and Lisa fussed with the strings of fairy lights that draped along the bushes separating the two properties. The feud between myself and my uncles didn't last long.

Once they saw that I was serious about moving back to Rose Hill and rebuilding my life here with Billy, they welcomed me with open arms. I think it helped that I gave them full access to the boathouse and the dock, which was all Paul really wanted anyway. I even caved and continued to allow Lisa to include the house on the historical society's summer house tour. Now that I was around more, believe it or not, Lisa had kind of grown on me. We're not close and we're not friends, but we'd gotten used to each other and her voice no longer set my teeth on edge. Or at least not too much anyway.

Molly and I met up occasionally. She'd become a snow bird and spent her winters on the west coast of Florida where she met a very nice retired fireman. She still missed my mother terribly. But, Molly has her children and grandchildren along with her new companion so she was fine. Molly will always be fine.

I saw Sister Elizabeth at mass at St. Ann's and sometimes she would come back to the house with me afterwards for coffee. I imagined my mother laughing as she saw us sitting together. Me, the prodigal daughter. I didn't make mass every week, I wasn't that reformed, but I did go regularly. Billy would come with me sometimes. The quiet rituals, the smiling faces of the neighbors, hell even the hokey bake sales and other fundraisers, they all gave me comfort. Peace. I felt closer to my mother there, if that made any sense.

"There. See. Not too big, right?"

I turned to look at my daughter, her fiery curls tamed into an elegant chignon. She smiled. Her navy silk dress brought out the blue in her wide-set eyes.

"You did good, Laurie," I said to my old friend. "Her hair is perfect."

"You like it, hon?" she asked Veronica.

"Yeah." Veronica smiled. "I do."

"Are we allowed to see the bride yet?" My son Timmy boomed from the doorway.

"Well, look at you two." Michael and Timmy looked devastatingly handsome in their dark suits. Careful of my makeup, Timmy kissed me on the cheek.

Veronica picked up the two rose blossoms and stood on her toes to pin them to her brothers' lapels. My beautiful, beautiful children.

"Mom, are you ready?" Timmy asked.

"Can you give me a minute, sweetheart. I'll be right down."

"Sure, Mom."

I walked to the window. Below, the wedding guests began to assemble around the rose covered trestle under which I was to marry Billy. Billy, his hair trim and neat, stood under it, laughing with his brother Tommy. My brother Denis and his fiancé stood next to them. My brother Dom and his wife Alison walked hand in hand from the boathouse, carrying flutes of champagne. Other guests trickled from the boathouse. My uncles, some new friends from the SEC, and Auntie Maura's sons and their wives. Poor Maura didn't make it to Christmas after my mother died. It was a shame she missed this. She loved nothing more than a good wedding.

Molly and her boyfriend Karl leant against the garden gate. Once Molly had met Karl, some five years her junior and still fit from his years in the fire department, she kidded me that now she too had found her boy toy. At first I was insulted that she had dared call my Billy a boy toy. This was the man who had poured love like oil onto my dried out husk of a life. He loved and adored me in every way possible and after the emotional desert of my marriage and the turmoils of my mother's last few months, I drank it in. In so many ways, he brought me back to life.

And, yet.

And yet, I couldn't discuss my cases at the SEC with him the way I could with Brendan. Billy didn't share my love of reading or of music. I'd never seen him read a paper other than the sports pages and I didn't think he'd ever sat through an entire newscast. I brought him to a work dinner at Le Cirque in the city and while it wasn't a complete disaster, it wasn't exactly a success. Brendan had his faults, but he fit into my world. Maybe not the world I grew up in, but the world I created with my diplomas and my aspirations. What world did Billy fit into?

I moved away from the window and walked to my vanity. In the heart shaped crystal jewelry box that Billy gave me last Valentine's day lay my mother's St. Brigid's cross on its delicate silver chain. I carefully lifted it and draped it around my neck. I wondered what my mother would think of my marriage. And Kitty. I remembered asking my grandmother once if she would ever get married again. She laughed. "Not if he were hung with gold, love. Not if he were hung with gold."

I fixed my lipstick and blotted it on a tissue, as I had seen my grandmother do with such panache so many times. Billy may not be hung with gold, but he was here. He would always be here if I let him. That may not be everything, but maybe it was enough.

The string quartet began to play. I lifted my mother's cross to my lips and slowly walked down the stairs.

The End

Bernadette Walsh is a native New Yorker who, when she isn't busy practicing law and tormenting her fellow commuters on the Long Island Rail Road with the tap-tap-tapping of her laptop, enjoys reading and now writing novels. As the daughter of an Irish immigrant, she has always been fascinated by the Irish immigrant experience and explores some of these themes in The Girls on Rose Hill. Bernadette has won several writing contests. The Girls on Rose Hill is her sixth published novel. Kensington Publishing has published five of her other titles: Gold Coast Wives, and the four books of her paranormal series, The Devlin Legacy (comprised of Devil's Mountain; Devil's Shore; Devil's Daughter; and The Devlin Witch). Bernadette's books are available on most e-retailer sites.

Bernadette also hosts a show on blogtalkradio, Nice Girls Reading Naughty Books, where she interviews various members of the publishing industry. In 2013 Bernadette was named a "featured host" by blogtalkradio.

Further information about Bernadette's books and radio show can be found at www.bernadettewalsh.com.

Table of Contents

Made in United States
North Haven, CT
17 March 2022

17227069R00105